IN UZ

Charles Brownson

other crime fiction by Charles Brownson

Ancestors (Jump River Press, 1984)

Library of Congress Cataloging in Publication data

Brownson, Charles, 1945-

    In Uz.

I. Title.

PS3552.R788U9   813.54
ISBN 0-89472-012-0

The past is a foreign country. They do things differently there.

—L.P. Hartley

A mud floor, like a mercenary marriage, does certainly promote early rising.

--Alexander Kinglake

We understand the characters of people who do not interest us.

—Marcel Proust

There are two kinds of crimes that keep the imagination the crime hero and the crime mystery, all the other crimes everybody forgets as soon as they find out who did them.

—Gertrude Stein

IN UZ

One Friday evening toward the end of July, Caitlin Vachon received a telephone call from her former employer James Porres. He had expanded his business and wanted an accountant.

Nothing on the side, he assured her. The regular thing. Retainers, hourly rates.

James, how can I work both for you and the bank? Your own bank. Conflict of interest.

You always moonlighted for Bill, didn't you?

Shoebox accounts, James. You know Bill kept a firm for his regular business. Why don't you use them? They know the books.

I don't like them. I want a change. Everything of Bill's is going out.

How bright and hard he sounded. Caitlin had to hold the telephone just a little away from her ear. How unlike the dark, soft days of the partnership with Bill.

He had begun to absorb Bill's business, it seemed. What was he using for money?

Full time, then, he sputtered. On the payroll, Caitlin. Stop in and see me on Monday.

No.

Then I'll come over. Will you be home?

She sighed. All right.

Monday night. Eight o'clock.

The connection was cleanly broken. Caitlin sighed again and hung the dead telephone handset in its place on the wall. Where had he called from? There had been voices in the background: the store? No, he had always hated evening hours. No evening hours. No hubbub.

What did Porres want with her now? She was Bill's protege, wasn't she? Did he think she could do him any harm? Was he trying to buy her off?

1

Perhaps. On Monday night he sat in her tiny apartment and talked too much. He held out a lot of left-handed apologies which he was too cautious or too embarrassed, or just too timid to simply put down on the table for her, like a house gift. He only wanted to be sure she understood. That he hadn't been responsible for. That he had, in fact, tried to. That he had never thought to wash his hands of.

He had, though. She was sure of it.

He was getting hold of himself, making a new life. Admirable.

Really, he had changed remarkably. She had been fond of him once. Why should she find it so hard now to forgive him? Disgusting behavior.

She couldn't accept the job, of course. He had known that all along. The offer had been for old times, then. Old times that he was otherwise doing his best to cover up and forget.

Remembering, he stayed late. She gave him sherry, curious because what he remembered bore only a little resemblance to what she had heard before from Bill, from Lieutenant Crake and the others.

Would there ever be agreement upon these things?

He drank too much sherry, out of control, intimate. He was going to go on living alone, would sell the house and rent a duplex on Ash: an old place, cool, shaded by eucalyptus and a huge old olive, only a few blocks from the shop. Isela had gone to her sister's. In Douglas, of all places. Almost a ghost town. Miners, yes. It was something of a mystery to him what his ex-wife would do. She had nothing to sell . . .

□

There was already a small crowd around the door when Milo Crake arrived. Just once he would have liked to go unobtrusively to work without the uniformed officers attracting a crowd, without having to push his way in, without the whispering. It was a spurious notoriety, the sort of thrill that volunteer rescue squads like. He recalled liking it himself, as a young man.

Tuchman, the responding officer, was the sort who likes to

brief his superiors at every opportunity, another annoyance. There was no need to offend the man, of course. But there was no need to listen, either. Simply let him talk, let him take a hit of his own peculiar bi-valent drug. Fawning. Self-important. Everyone is, sometimes.

Besides the uniformed officer there were two others in the bookstore. James Porres he knew, a paunchy little bald-headed fellow, ridiculous in yellow jerseys and naked white legs. The other was a woman in business clothes. She sat at Porres's desk, dabbing at her nose with a bit of toilet paper but not otherwise appearing any more shocked than a sales girl who gets to work and finds the boss dead. The conditions of employment, my dear, are somewhat changed, I'm sorry to say. And such a long bus ride this morning, too, for naught. Porres looked as if he would like to stand a bit closer to her, either for comfort or to hide himself, but that would have brought him a little too close to the corpse of his past success, so he stayed where he was.

The former Laurence William Face lay on the floor in the aisle just beside the desk. A few papers, part of a stack on a corner of the desk, lay beside or somewhat under him. Out in the aisle lay a book, spine up, just beyond the reach of Face's outflung arm. There was a little blood spot, not directly under his head, which seemed to have come from a scalp wound. It looked very much as if he had slipped from the stock ladder and broken his neck.

Crake resisted an urge to peer at the book. He could see very well what it was without that, and the place on the shelf from which it had come, but unless he peered at things people thought he wasn't serious. A dog-eared novel. He would never understand how it was possible to sell a used novel, neither old nor beautiful, for twice the original price. The papers, however, he glanced at sufficiently to confirm his impression that they had been swept from the desk top in the fall. He tugged gently at one to verify that it was pinned beneath the body. There was a little blood on the corner of the desk. Face had apparently tried to rise once. But it was a clean job, with no thrashing about.

What time did the store close last night?

Five o'clock.

Porres's voice was about as unsteady as the Lieutenant had expected. Crake turned his attention to the woman.

My name is Caitlin Vachon, she said, not rising. Mr. Porres asked me to come.

Did he.

I work just down the street. I'm an analyst in the bank. Mr. Porres and I are good friends. I used to work here, when I was a student.

So the clothing and the self-possession were explained, and also the clerkish air which had led him to put her down as a shop girl. She was a shop girl, if he cared to look for excuses.

The dead man was dressed casually, in a knit shirt, jeans, and running shoes without socks.

Was Mr. Face in the habit of coming to the store after closing?

I haven't known him to do so, Porres replied, his voice still uncertain, as if there had recently been something stuck in his throat.

But he used to come in late? Milo Crake went on, remembering.

Yes, years ago. But not for some time now. Not since we stopped keeping the shop open evenings, at least.

Crake nodded. There was nothing to be done now until the medical people and the photographers were through. He eyed the telephone on the desk but, thinking better of it, went out to make his calls with the radio in Tuchman's patrol car. He had walked, himself, since police headquarters were just around the corner. There aren't many chances to walk to work anymore.

The crowd outside the shop had pretty well dispersed, perhaps convinced it was only a heart attack. Perhaps it was. Crake didn't think so. He sat in the patrol car with the door open, waiting for the forensic crew and thinking over what to do before lunch. The initial ruling would certainly be accidental death. But Crake was reluctant to accept that an athletic man like Bill Face, wearing rubber-soled shoes, could slip off the second or third step of a sturdy ladder and break his neck, in search of an inconsequential book, in the middle of the night.

Was he athletic? Looked it, that's all. Thin, ascetic.

There was another question: were the lights on? Perhaps he had been feeling around in the dark. Who goes to get a book in the dark?

Crake went back inside to scan the upper shelves near the desk. All second-hand novels. What Face had been after was simply stock, it seemed. Crake went out the back into the parking lot to look at Face's automobile, which was parked hastily at an angle, several feet from the wall. Returning inside, he looked over the crowded storeroom for some evidence that Face had been bumbling in the dark, but found none.

Which way did you come in this morning?

Porres had been persuaded to sit down. The Vachon woman, due at work herself, was making excuses. Crake shooed her out and, speculatively, watched her swing up the aisle.

Through the back, Porres said.

Was it locked?

Yes.

Milo Crake drummed his fingers with some impatience, wanting to know if Face's key was in his pocket but unable to disturb the corpse until forensics had finished with it.

Is it necessary to go through all of this, bleated Porres, for an accident?

Yes.

It wasn't, of course. A simple certificate would do, and some inquiries later. An autopsy. It was for Crake to decide. His doubts could be set aside. Officially set aside, at any rate.

Forensics showed up at last and so Tuchman was released to go and write up his report. Face's keys were in his pocket after all, along with the usual trinkets, so nothing was proved on that ground.

You haven't been robbed, have you, by the way?

Porres started. He ran his eyes quickly over the shelves—those opposite the desk, Crake noticed, rather than those behind it where Face had been prowling when he fell—and he looked into the till.

No, nothing has been taken.

Do you keep a flashlight?

Porres produced it from the desk. It failed to work. Crake

nodded, dismissing that point also.

He took up the book which Face had been getting off the shelf and bent the covers back, forcing the spine to stand up, making the joints crack, enjoying the antiquarian's grimace. But there was nothing tucked inside, nor did there appear to be anything glued under the flysheets or anywhere in the gutter. He put the book back on the shelf. Aside from its being a little taller than the others there was nothing to distinguish it. Crake supposed he ought to confiscate the thing, have the lab tear it apart.

That was interesting. The shelf on which the book belonged was too low to require a stock ladder to reach. Puzzled, Crake walked restlessly to the back of the shop and then again out onto the street. The police radio was blatting details of a pedestrian accident.

□

On Friday afternoon on his way back to the office, Milo Crake stopped by the bank to have a word with Caitlin. How convenient, he observed, to find you just coming out.

Isn't it.

They walked for a block in silence. She was one of those, he perceived, who see with the third eye that hidden but indelible stain, and who suspect the police whenever something has gone wrong. Perhaps she was simply intimidated by his size? He had gone a bit fat with age, too, which didn't help.

In the mews behind the shops on the next block was a tiny park just large enough for two benches, but the grass had recently been watered and the benches were wet. They were obliged to stand in the parking lot. Caitlin leaned on the fender of her car and Crake against the wall of the building. Eyes averted from each other, they gazed instead at the inaccessible little green swatch of grass.

The parks were Bill's idea, you know, said Caitlin at last. Largely his idea, at any rate.

Were they. And what did you have to do with the bookshop, then?

I worked there while I was in college.

The short walk, the languid April heat, had made her somewhat less brisk.

As a bookkeeper. Mr. Porres thought I'd taken an interest in the business. He offered to let me try my hand at a catalog.

Is that a great test?

No, but the catalog goes out to collectors, you see, who are quite knowledgeable. The annotations are a chance to show off one's scholarship. And it must have some unity, balance. It can't be just a list—

She broke off, vexed to have her reserve so easily breached, vexed by the detective's smile.

She was young, wasn't she? Long out of college?

A year.

You've kept up contact, haven't you.

Yes.

I wouldn't have thought the bookshop would need an accountant.

A shoebox account. I was just a student.

A favor, then.

Yes, I suppose so.

You didn't do any of Face's books.

Other than for the shop? No, of course not.

Ah. The detective's expression seemed to grow more cynical.

He wanted to look at her keys. They were in a side pocket of her purse, a little ring of three with a big plastic tag and a metal whistle attached.

What do you know of Face's business? he asked, returning the keys without comment.

Very little. I wouldn't expect to. There was nothing irregular.

You know of nothing irregular.

That's right.

And Porres knew of your relations with his partner?

Why shouldn't he know?

Now Crake's smile was broad, avuncular, without a trace of sarcasm. Bill Face would have enjoyed this woman. She was well-made, firm, neither luxurious nor spare. And she dressed well, but not severely, which showed self-confidence: good leather walking shoes, soft maroon pants, and an eccentric blouson shirt with puffed sleeves and a flaming scarf tie. Long legs, supple waist, loose blond hair and a small Welsh face that fit her name . . .

Crake returned his gaze to the wet park grass that was not enough to pitch a tent on, with its little border of some white-flowered herb. He felt some tenderness, of the sort that had been more common when his daughter was small, a simple-minded goodwill which his two sons, coming afterward, had never roused to the same degree. And it had all disappeared eventually, of course.

It was just five o'clock. After he left Caitlin, Crake decided to retrace his steps and look in on someone else before going home. According to the posted sign, Rufus Woyke, Bookseller, did business until six. But the store was empty and the clerk, who did not seem pleased at Crake's entrance, occupied himself with some books which were not standing neatly enough on the shelf.

Excuse me.

The clerk was a sandy-haired young man with a sharp nose, vaguely familiar to the Lieutenant. But at Crake's age it seemed as if everyone was vaguely familiar.

Excuse me.

Crake despised theatrical detectives who did not go straight to work. As if he had stopped by for something to read on the bus and had only just remembered the murder of poor Mr. Dobson which had had him stumped for a week now. Or the reverse, ostentatiously inspecting the premises, and the doorknobs with particular care, with a big show of badges and papers at the end.

Excuse me. I'd like to speak to the proprietor.

I am he, Lieutenant Crake. I am he.

What an irritating surprise.

Rufus Woyke shrugged his narrow shoulders. As you see, I have nothing to do but tidy the shelves and stare out the window. You make no effort to conceal your identity. I presume you have come about the death of my colleague.

Bill Face. Yes.

Woyke left off his nervous tinkering with the arrangement of his stock and turned to face the detective. He was strikingly homely.

Say on.

The man's ugliness gave unusual force to his blunt speech. Lieutenant Crake blinked, recovered.

How long have you been in this location, Mr. Woyke?

Three years.

And how long in the business?

The same.

Here are two bookstores in the same block. You are the new-comer. How did you imagine this would be a good spot?

You blame my inexperience, Lieutenant. But I was invited here.

And Face didn't object to the competition?

Woyke's smile was peculiarly coy. The invitation, I should say, was from William himself. So you see, we are not competitors. William would hardly have permitted that. James does not sell new books, as you have noticed.

You are in financial difficulties, I believe.

My business is for sale.

Shouldn't books sell pretty well here?

You would think so.

Near a university and all. They seem to manage across the street.

Yes, they seem to. Woyke paused long enough to allow the other meaning of his words to bubble up.

But you see, he went on, James's trade is not local.

It has been.

Yes, hasn't it?

Despite appearances, as you say, Mr. Woyke. Face was chronically short of cash. How far in arrears are you?

Six months.

And your, ah, invitation? It hasn't been withdrawn?

Woyke laughed, or perhaps snorted. You are plainly ignorant of your quarry, Lieutenant. William was not a dunning man. He had other means of raising money to remedy what was, after all, an ordinary cash flow problem. He would have thought it in poor taste to mention my arrears. I assure you I have not been forced out. It was simple incompetence, sir.

How long does your lease run?

Three years more.

Very liberal of him.

Typically so. Liberality is a privilege of the wealthy. You suggest that William was impecunious, but this is only a ruse of yours to justify an inquiry into my affairs.

Crake saw no reason to deny this. You are well informed about your employer's affairs, he observed.

Not my employer, Lieutenant. My landlord.

What do you know of relations between Face and Porres?

Woyke gave half a smile. I think I shall close early today, he said, and turned his back.

Woyke ambled toward the rear of the store, pausing to adjust yet another rack of books. After a time the lights went out. Then the swamp cooler was shut off and immediately the silent store began to seem stuffy. Outside it was already dark. Woyke re-emerged from the gloom to lock the street door, then turned his attention to emptying the cash register. The cash was meager, and he did not trouble to count it.

William had a great many proteges, he said, as if to himself. James is one of them, perhaps the first. William would never abandon anyone to the fate he deserved. He was one of the few to fully appreciate gratitude as a source of power. And William had a great deal of power. But it would be an injustice to say that he was only interested in acquiring an entourage. His ambitions were much loftier than that, than the role of the well-heeled playboy which he cultivated so assiduously. He was a philanthropist. He was a competitor. He was angered by injustice, by constraints, by lack of opportunity. His natural adversary, his only worthy adversary, was fate. James Porres is his creation, and a quite good example of William's ability to devise unnatural destinies.

Woyke dropped the money into a bank bag, leaving the pennies in the open drawer. Crake speculatively jingled the keys in his pocket and gazed across the street, where Porres was still at work in his own shop.

There are others, of course.

Eh?

Woyke smiled indulgently. I was speaking of William's creatures. The Vachon woman was quite an innocent little thing when she came to us. But William's virtue soon repaired that. Innocent people do such harm.

Ah?

My hat, said Woyke, and vanished into the back. Crake waited, keeping well out of sight of the window, and at length Woyke returned. When they were out on the street, Crake set off without another word, briskly toward headquarters.

Awfully warm for a hat, he muttered after a block.

□

James Porres was a man who measured his commute to work in inches and tried to imagine the sound of three miles of guitar string; a man who knew in detail the lives of passe writers, the struggles of obscure translators, the publishers' returns on all editions of *Nineveh and Its Remains*. He would have preferred to run his business from a post office box, which he could well do if he were free of the shop which Bill insisted on. He had built up the more congenial antiquarian side over the years (travel and translated literature were his specialties) until now he could have lived without going out.

He lived on Greenway Drive, 197683 inches from work. It was not difficult to measure: some 2300 revolutions of the wheels of his bicycle were required to get him to work, and each revolution carried him forward 86 inches. He did the calculation in his head one morning a few days after buying the bicycle. After that he amused himself by finding the mid-point of the trip, and the rest of the first dozen harmonics, and the points of a scale, just as if the way to work were a wire strung taut between Greenway Drive and the bookshop, a string which he supposed, if it could somehow be plucked, would sound a note so deep it would shake the roots of the earth.

The bicycle was his doctor's idea. He had been riding all winter and it was true that he had begun to feel fit. Besides which

he no longer had trouble finding a parking place downtown. Of
course, there was always a vacant place in the little lot behind
the shop that Bill parked in, which Porres would have liked to
leave free for customers. So the bicycle was a convenience. But
now the weather was turning hot again. Porres could not expect
to play three-mile scales in a coat and tie in a hundred ten degrees and arrive pale and crisp.

It was mid-April. The street along the way to work was fret-
ted at hundreds of points and Porres had begun to compose
eerie little rising tunes for himself, varying the principle of
composition from day to day. When the string was stopped at
the third palm tree past Hermosa Drive, that was an F#, or a
C# in the second octave if he listened for the fifth partial. All
the palm trees in succession yielded a siren. The sequence of
frets marked by street signs could be made to yield a pizzicato
which was a distant echo of the opening of Bartok's violin con-
certo. And so as the summer came on this aeolian music that
sounded in the wake of Porres's bicycle grew in beauty and
complexity, and Porres began to think of symphonies. Perhaps
he could ride through the summer after all, if he kept an extra
suit and some fresh shirts in the lavatory at the store. He would
need some riding shorts.

Over the lunch hour on Friday he walked down the street to
the sporting goods store and tried on some yellow nylon shorts.
He could hardly bring himself to come out of the dressing room
to look at himself in the mirror. He may have felt fit, but he
didn't look it. More of a suntan would help, he thought. Here
it was April. He was still as pale as paper. But he had lost
twenty pounds, at least.

Even Bill Face had said he looked better. In twenty years of
business partnership, that was the first piece of unqualified
praise Porres had heard from him.

Monday was slow. Bill, typically, did not come in. Several
times they had talked about closing the shop on Mondays, but
as it cost them nothing to be open, nothing was done. Someone
else might have preferred to do nothing at home, in the swimming pool, but Porres preferred to sit undisturbed in the silence
of his own shop, going leisurely through the catalogs of other

dealers, enjoying the smell of the books and watching the pass-
ersby on the street outside.

He did not think he would get much thinner after all. It was
more comfortable to be frumpy. Just a little frumpy. From
the comfort of darkness he gazed out into the bright street at
the crowd of students. The money and glamour of these children disconcerted him. Cars, clothes, three pairs of roller skates,
sun-tanned testicles.

It would be better, he thought, if the shop were not quite so
trendy in appearance. What was to distinguish it from Woyke's
shop across the street? There should be more books and less
light, and not so much old brick and barn wood, and Porres
himself should be something more of a hedgehog. Yellow athletic jerseys were not the hedgehog style. They were more Bill's
spider style. Let Bill play the spider. The shop was a prime
business location, and to have that they had to have the rug and
barn wood and the uncluttered shelves. The whole downtown
reconstruction was Bill Face's doing. Now some thirty buildings, on both sides of the street, had been rebuilt as warrens of
small shops and restaurants, law offices, consulting firms. And
Bill had set the trendy tone, risked the first money. If it had
been left up to a hedgehog things would have gone very differently. But he had risen along with Bill, to some extent. Bill
had brought his partner up with him.

Porres poured himself another cup of coffee and picked up
the latest *Publisher's Weekly*. Caitlin emerged from the back
room and dropped a stack of paper on his desk on the way out.

I was in over the weekend, she said as she walked backwards
toward the door. The annotations are done. I'll be back in a
couple of days to type it up.

She turned, skipping, and blundered into a display of boxed
paperbacks. Adroitly catching them as they fell, she tumbled
them back onto the table and danced out. The mullions in the
door buzzed as they were wont to do when it was slammed, and
the bell clucked once.

A bell on a string that tinkled when the door was opened was
Bill's one concession to tradition, the romance of the ideal bookshop. When Porres went up to the front to set up again the dis-

play that Caitlin had knocked over, he reached up and flicked the bell to hear the clear, thin note it sang when it was not yanked so violently.

After Caitlin had gone, Porres browsed through the sheets of yellow legal paper she had left. It was the material for a new catalog, and Caitlin's own, her first. Sound work, he thought. Talent breeds in strange places. She had come to them as a bookkeeper, an economics student in need of money. Now she worked for a bank, but she had developed a taste for the book business, it seemed, for she had persuaded Porres to let her do a catalog from stock. He hadn't resisted much. He wondered if she would still do their accounts, too, in her spare time. Bill's accountant complained about that, and always had.

Probably she had other reasons for hanging around. Women usually did, where Bill was concerned.

□

So Porres was becoming a businessman. He had offered her employment.

Caitlin watched him go away down the hall toward the stairs: short, half bald, excruciatingly cautious James Porres. When he had gone, she closed the apartment door and leaned back against it, her eyes closed.

Deep down, she did not believe in change. At the bottom of her stomach, as indigestible as unleavened bread, lay the idea that change is only an illusion. A pigeon is flushed from an empty hat and the wide-eyed child shouts in glee, even though she knows it is a trick. It must be, mustn't it? But she didn't know how the trick was done, innocent and anxious little thing that she was, and feared the time when she would have to complain that it was a damned cheat.

Her mother's face reddened. Ss.

James Porres had become cold and hard since Bill's death. But he had always been like this, hadn't he? He'd just been keeping it under his hat. She was mistaken before, when Crake produced his pigeon. No doubt she was mistaken now.

She would probably always be ignorant, always innocent.

As a girl, a guilty adolescent, Caitlin was troubled by an absence of answers to questions she now thought a little silly: Why is there anything? Why should I? Those questions were eventually punctured somehow, and the mystery leaked out of them, much as it had from an earlier set of questions that were never answered either: Why is water wet? Why do you love me? Preoccupied as she always was with getting started, she hardly ever noticed how old questions were abandoned when they were no longer interesting. She thought she was getting on, leaving them behind. But she was only wandering distractedly, pulling out a welter of scarves and pigeons and apples without finding anything interesting.

It was late. She had laundry to do before work in the morning. It was late and dark and hot. The dust storm that earlier smudged the sunset had now subsided, leaving the air close. Caitlin turned off the air conditioner and opened the bedroom window. The city smelled of scorched grass, hot metal, ozone. These odors, so characteristic—the smell of the electronics assembly plants, the rolling mill on the other side of the park, of dry desert earth—seemed to be stirred up, intensified, by a dust storm. Caitlin stripped to a t-shirt, turned on the bedside fan, and lay down on a bed naked of sheets or pillow. The laundry could wait.

So. Porres had become a businessman.

Everything of Bill's going out, he had said.

She sat up. The books. Bill's accounts. Going out.

On Monday morning, still in her underwear, she called Porres to say she might reconsider.

He was still in his old shop. Afterward, she crossed the street to look in the window of Rufus Woyke's bookstore. Re-opening soon under new management, said a placard taped to the glass. Alongside the store ran a passageway, now barred by a gate, which led into an interior courtyard of the building where a warren of small shops sold sandals, used records, cookies, counseling retreats in the San Francisco Mountains. Caitlin stepped back into the shadow in the mouth of the passage and leaned against the grate. From the shadows, she watched Porres lock up.

Lieutenant Crake, it was Caitlin's opinion, had been an acute but essentially instinctive man, unaccustomed to and perhaps incapable of rigorous proof. She doubted that proof had ever been required of him. Perhaps he even disbelieved in the possibility of it. So many of his cases were perfectly obvious, yielded so easily to a little pressure at the right points. Police work, she thought, must be mostly an instinct for the right points. And any leftover cases were insoluble, senseless, accidental, mad. Every once in a while luck must create a perfect crime out of incomprehensible motives, missing evidence, stupid or uncooperative witnesses. Crake had thumped everything to see what was hollow, what could be cracked, broken open. More was never necessary. Porres might be the first hollow man to come out whole.

Perhaps there really was nothing more to be learned. Perhaps things were as they seemed: incoherent, broken. Perhaps it was possible, after all, to explain things without explaining them away.

□

James Porres began to lock up the shop. He was still thinking about the draft of the sale catalog that Caitlin had prepared, wondering what to do with it. Why should he encourage her? He didn't want help anyway. The beneficent mood of earlier in the day had evaporated.

When he got home he found that Isela had spent the day chewing and refining a number of complaints against him, which had become so dense as to be indigestible. Caught unprepared, Porres defended himself with whatever came to hand, but he only succeeded in annoying her. The argument continued to grow all evening, a malignant syllogism constructed with cancerous logic, and in the morning he woke up with a sore throat, as if he had been arguing in his sleep.

Isela did not get up for breakfast. Their daughter Soccorro acted as go-between, over granola and bagels.

It's about the vacation, Soccorro explained.

Vacation? What has she said about a vacation? Nothing.

Well, Daddy, she thinks you won't want to go.

Of course I won't want to.

He goggled. Soccorro lowered her gaze on the pretext of spreading jam on her second toasted bagel. His daughter could eat what she liked, while he had begun to scrimp breakfast. Soccorro filled her mouth with cereal. They gazed at each other across the table until Porres discovered they were chewing in unison. He swallowed hastily, gulped some coffee, and turned sideways on his chair.

Every spring it was the same argument with his wife. It was probably written on the calendar. Start fight with James today.

Isela wanted to go somewhere cool. Porres wanted to stay in the shop. In their first years, when the business was shaky, the moral strength had been all on his side. Now he had nothing to defend but a tradition of staying home and no defense but some aesthetic complaints about Michigan and other places where Isela wanted to go. But he had nevertheless so far prevailed. If it were only a question of the ability to endure sieges, he could hardly fail.

You know, Porres said, ostentatiously gazing into his coffee cup, I have always thought your mother surprisingly intolerant of the heat. For a native. I've thought of keeping a little record, to find out the temperature which sets her off on this vacation humbug every year. I suppose the newspapers have been thrown out? What is the forecast?

Daddy, you're always trying to find some biological explanation.

I'm a complete determinist, Porres replied complacently. Psychology is out. Biology is in.

Ethics is out, too?

Extinct. The whole fungus family is endangered, in fact. Politics and religion are the only mushrooms left in the forest.

Phylum.

Eh?

Species genus family order class phylum. Fungi are a phylum.

An esoteric error. Porres strove to look downcast. Soccorro giggled. He admonished her with his spoon, flicking little drops of milk into her face as he spoke.

You tell your mother . . .

Daddy, stop!

You tell your mother that on the first day it gets over one hundred and five . . .

He replenished his spoon in the milk. Soccorro caught him on the cheek with a glob of marmalade from her knife.

The very day the temperature breaks a hundred five we are going to Michigan.

He added a little cereal to the catapult. Soccorro tore off bits of buttered bagel for ammunition.

You tell her— But he was laughing too hard now to give a connected ultimatum. Soccorro took refuge behind her chair.

Tell her to be packed and ready—he knelt, laughing, to shoot under the table—to be ready the moment the artichokes wilt— he rested his cheek on the cool tiles, holding his sides—

What the hell is this?

It was Isela, in her nightshirt and flip-flops, standing in the kitchen doorway. On the floor, Porres and Soccorro lay giggling. Soccorro's face glistened. There was milk on the table and on the walls and Porres's shirt was spotted with butter and marmalade.

I'm evolving, he gasped.

What? It's a stupid food fight.

Porres struggled to his feet. His nose was running. Giggling, sniffling, working out of his spoiled shirt, he kissed his astonished wife's nose and went upstairs to dress.

It's Tuesday, he mumbled. We always have evolution on Tuesday. And on the way to work he played the ground bass of the earth with such vigor and concentration that he was nearly run over by a car at College and Broadway.

That afternoon Bill Face came into the shop, letting himself in through the delivery entrance as usual. The store was empty of customers. Porres sat at his desk amid a stack of reference books and catalogs. Saying nothing, Face poured himself a cup of coffee from the pot which always stood near the desk.

Bill used to say of his coffee cup, in a time when he spent more time around the shop, that it was his representative. If you need my vote, he would say, you ask this mug. Do whatever it tells you and I'll back it one hundred percent. This mug knows the business.

He seemed a little rumpled this afternoon, as if he had been up all night. His light blue suit was wrinkled in odd places and, though he was shaved and perfumed as usual, his eyes were dark. He poured a cup of coffee and ambled to the front of the store, where he leaned against the shelves in a corner and looked out from the shadows into the sunlit street.

I'm going to take some vacation this year, Porres ventured. Who is there to look after the shop during June?

Bill turned away from the window, putting the light behind him. Are you taking only June? he returned with a mocking lilt. How compulsive, James.

Yes, I suppose Isela will want more, won't she?

What about Caitlin Vachon? You think she has a head for the business, I'm told.

Who said so?

Bill shrugged. You liked her work on the new catalog?

Yes. How do you know that?

And how should I not know it, James?

She has a full-time job. Perhaps she might like to come in on a Saturday, but I hardly think she could arrange more.

Bill nodded, as if he had forgotten that Caitlin was no longer a student. He took a slow drink of coffee and turned back to the window.

In earlier days Caitlin had kept the shop open one or two evenings a week. Before that it was Bill himself who worked late, presided over readings, made the shop a night spot for a few surreptitiously odd persons among the respectable students of law, engineering, and business. But the shop no longer sold trade books, or kept evening hours, or sponsored poetry readings, and Bill had turned his attention to other things. It was less usual now for him to know of such things as Caitlin's work on the new catalog. In the year since Caitlin there had been a few others, none of whom pleased Porres. They didn't steal; they didn't care enough to. Porres preferred to manage by himself.

What about Luther Idge? he suggested, meaning Rufus Woyke's assistant in the shop across the street.

No.

That was abrupt.

I'll come in myself, said Bill, softening after a little. It won't hurt me to breathe morning air, will it? It doesn't seem to have damaged you any?

It will— hm. Porres's voice faltered. It will be all right, Bill. Perhaps we could just close up for a month. Business will be slow in June. There never are many legs then.

Bill finished his coffee and walked back to replace the cup. He didn't reply, but smiled with his familiar acidity. To Porres he seemed tired. He went out through the back room without another word.

Porres sighed and washed up the cup.

□

Unlike Porres, Caitlin did not remember Bill Face as he had been, as he was reported to have been, at twenty, and so she didn't think the change in him surprising. For one thing, unlike Porres he never appeared to age. She found old photographs of him: news stories from student days, in the student paper; his senior picture in the yearbook now defunct; publicity photographs in the newspaper from the first stages of the downtown rehabilitation project. He had remained lean, had kept his thick black hair and his twisted smile. At forty he grew a moustache but that hardly changed him, or softened the glint that she noticed even in a smudged newsprint portrait.

But there had been a metamorphosis nevertheless. The bohemian poet and radical became somehow the entrepreneur and politician of forty. At what age is the character finally formed? Or is it that our souls are bartered away in the womb, leaving only unrusting aluminum? If Porres seemed to Caitlin not enough of a piece then Bill Face was nearly seamless. There must have been a crack somewhere, a fault, if she would look closely enough. Why did Bill remake himself, after all, but that he discovered in himself a crack: a love of action and power? Didn't that explain everything?

Isela Porres had known Bill for a long time: longer than her husband had known him, longer than her husband. Had known the cracks and crevices like some anemone, a soft fleshy flower which feels the rock over for a hold and, catching it, grows inward— Caitlin would have to be careful not to pry so deeply as that or she would have to be cut loose at the end.

Why did you marry James?

Bill always wanted to know why, too. Whenever he spotted some scrap of useful information, which he saved like bits of string, he began that tenacious, maddening cross-examination.

Isela rolled over to reach the wine glass standing on the bedside table. James didn't quite turn out, she said, feeling defeated by both of them.

More wine?

No.

Caitlin set her empty glass down on the patio floor beside her chair. Why had Isela consented to talk to her? For the same reasons that Caitlin had told James she would do his books?

But she wouldn't, really. She was not going to get in that far.

They've made up their minds, haven't they? said Isela, meaning the police. She raised her head slightly from the chaise where she was sunbathing to look at Caitlin. So inconvenient for them, to have to take up that old business again. One simply hates these people who keep coming back, who never like any answer they're given. Neurotics. And you're a woman, too. They must hate it, your asking them to look into the business of Bill's death again.

Isela fell back on the chaise and lay for a time ruminating, swirling the ice cube slowly around the bottom of her glass. Caitlin said nothing. She had no intention of asking the police to reopen the case.

But of course, you're curious. It never hurts to satisfy a woman's curiosity, does it?

Isela roused herself to get a refill from the decanter of orange juice on the patio table. The juice had made her voice somewhat husky. Leaning forward, straddling the chaise, Isela now spoke with a little less studied weariness. Caitlin listened with eyes downcast, fixed on the fringe of black hair which escaped in ragged curls from under the edge of the older woman's white bikini.

Oh, I was very young. Several years younger than you, I should think. My family was poor. Poor people are insecure. A poor woman's chances are so few, don't you know, and beauty is so fleeting. I was a bit hasty. And James was already established in business. He was gentle, comfortable, even witty. All quite common. Not the sordid sort of mistake that one makes now, is it?

Caitlin said nothing. Her gaze dropped farther, to Isela's feet. City feet, tanned in stripes by sandals, white toes gnarled by narrow shoes, with thick red nails. The soft, mocking voice went on, no longer requiring the little nudges of courtesy to keep it going.

Young women are so very canny now, aren't they? So determined to be wise, to dispense with comfort and security and love. One finds that, when everything has been arranged for, when one's comfort and security are assured, it's too late for ambition. One regrets not having taken a few chances, doesn't one? I don't suppose I need to tell *you* how a woman could have found herself in Bill's bed, do I? Don't protest, my dear— give me some credit for intelligence. My own daughter gave me that much. Why should I have objected to what other little cunny he may have found for himself? There was enough to go around. I was in no position to object. Why do women come to themselves so late?

Things began very well, you know. James had some knowledge of the trade and Bill had a talent for promotion. It was when Bill turned his hand to this renovation project that things went bad. That was when he began to feel his power. He was still young, he was magnetic, just enough along to escape the war protest and all that waste of time, so that when the others began to drift back again he was ten years ahead of them. They had to come to him then for what they wanted: money, influence, a chance to get into the game. How galling that must have been for Rufus Woyke and the others. What a strange little man Rufus was. I wonder that the police never suspected him. I suppose we're too sophisticated now to think anything of someone skulking about in black, with his hat pulled down, and all that.

Bill began to come into himself then, as I say, and that was when James began to show up so poorly. They would fight, you know, quietly, for days. Bill wanted to pull all the resources out of the store, gut it. He did, too. Bill wasn't a man to oppose on something of that sort. That was when I began to see the mistake I'd made. James never aspired to anything more than what he had, you know. We were married two years at the time.

Why didn't you get a divorce, then? Caitlin inquired. You had no children, no property.

My dear, I would have had no standing. I would have become the predatory woman, don't you see.

Did you know that James has bought up Woyke's competition?

Yes. Unnerving, isn't it? They must have twisted James's balls a bit too much when they had him up. Changed his personality. Become a business man. At his age.

Had him up?

The police, my dear. Isela looked away toward the swimming pool. On the other side, where the sun reached up to the condominium wall, a pale young man lay reading. The pool sweep hunted its way around the edge, tapping against the tiles.

Some sort of middle-age crisis, I suppose, Isela said at last. It won't hold up, because James has never had courage. I could never get him to go out to a club, or anything of that sort. He didn't know how to behave. He worried that he'd make a fool of himself. When we went to Mexico on holiday weekends he would starve rather than go into a restaurant. He would have to speak that broken Spanish of his, you know, and appear ridiculous. I had to drag him out of the house. For fifteen years we never had a decent vacation. He hated to travel.

□

Isela dropped her empty wine glass onto the rug beside the bed. Bill lay on his back. She combed the hair on his chest with her fingers.

We could go away, couldn't we? For a couple of weeks?

I suppose, Bill replied absently. The Yucatan. He moved her hand away.

You're tense.

Mmm.

What is it? Has something gone sour?

Mm. The city's bond issue is being held up. One vote lacking in the IDA.

She waited, but in vain. At last she rolled him over and began to knead his shoulders.

Whose vote?

Foster. Old-timey political boss. Big stomach, chews cigars, hates to give anything away.

Is there anything I can do?

She felt him stiffen, but that was soon under control.

No. He wants patronage for some creature of his on the Council. A contribution to the campaign fund. But no one wants to put up the money.

Take up a collection. How much does he want?

Mmm. The resistance is principled, strange as that may seem. I would put the money up myself, just to get things moving, except that all my loose change is tied up in this thing already. I'll have to liquidate something, I suppose. That means another round with your husband. James doesn't seem to grasp the working of venture capital. If this reconstruction project goes through there will be other resources. He can be as big or as little as he likes, then.

Bill—

To hell with it. Let's go out. It's only ten o'clock.

He rolled over, throwing her, and before she could protest had thrust his tongue into her, stopping all argument.

You used to like that, didn't you? Isela said. You'd do anything for that, wouldn't you, my dear? Oh, I thought I was being turned inside out. I just lost all control, don't you know.

Her voice died as she gazed away over the pool, and she began to tap the bottom of her glass against the leg of the aluminum chaise. The pale young sunbather had gone in, leaving a crumpled towel lying with one corner dipped in the softly lapping water.

This particular time, I remember, after we had gone out Bill found that he hadn't brought any cash. Typical. How many dinners did you stand him, my dear, because of that? He simply couldn't be bothered, could he? This was the sixties, you know, before they'd invented the automatic teller. The only thing open was the Circle K. You can't imagine what a pain it was in those days to get money in the middle of the night. There were plenty of places where he was known, of course, where he had credit--

Again Isela's voice trailed off. I did love him, you know, she said after a time. I think I know what that means.

Then she took up the thread again briskly. At any rate, it was the simplest thing all around to stop by the store and take something out of the till, and that was what we did. Then, just to avoid an argument, Bill would alter the tally by so much, you know. I suppose that after so long it began to be routine. You could hardly call it illegal, though I suppose it did have an effect on his taxes. And it gave him a freer hand, didn't it? So many unpleasant explanations were avoided that way.

Caitlin felt herself flush as she realized the implications of what Isela was saying. How long, she managed to ask, did this go on?

Why, the whole time, my dear.

Isela looked at her in momentary surprise, and then burst out laughing. You didn't know, did you? You poor dear, I suppose that was why he always left the books to you, because he thought you wouldn't notice it so readily. And I thought it was all for you. Well, you needn't feel bad. The professionals didn't notice it, either.

Caitlin gagged, enraged. Somehow she rose and, she supposed, made some strangled conventional excuse for her behavior. In those few seconds, no doubt, she gave Isela Porres much amusement.

Outside, the sprinklers had come on, cooling the air. Caitlin stopped for a moment on the walk to take a few breaths and wait for the blood to sink from her head. Stepping off the curb then, she re-entered the familiar night-time heat. She stretched, smiled. The slight headache, the swollen feeling which air-conditioning always caused, melted away.

It ought to be corroborated, of course. Would have to be. She unlocked her car, leaned in to roll down the windows, waited for the stale air inside to blow away with the new little erratic breeze.

Why, she wondered, resting her elbows on top of her car, did she instinctively believe anything malicious? Was everyone like that? She had an ungovernable and quite irrational suspicion that ill fortune is always deserved, good fortune gratuitous, a compliment false.

□

The coroner's report was on his desk Friday morning, but Crake did not sit down to look at it until Monday. Friday he went hunting, as he said: a somewhat wistful interview with the Vachon woman and another with the degenerate Rufus Woyke. When he returned to his desk after hours the report was in his basket, as he had known it would be. The usual 48-hour service. He left it there and went home.

But on Monday the report could not be put off. It was on his desk, sticking out from under some forms, neatly tabbed and legible even upside down: Face, Laurence William.

Crake was too accustomed to the unblinking analysis of motive not to know why he disliked opening that report. He knew he should not have been on this case to begin with. He should have left it to his subordinates when the call came in. But it had been a Wednesday, and he had wanted some air . . .

And then he had seen the case and known it was his, whether he wanted it or not. It might have been his good fortune to retire without working this particular murder, but he had never been a man given to regrets, or to avoiding work. What he dreaded now was that the coroner would have reported accidental death—death by mischance—and that he, Crake, would have to conduct an unofficial, perhaps illegal, investigation.

Milo Crake stretched out his hand and tweaked the brown folder from the middle of the pile. By instinct and long familiarity he turned to the paragraph which he knew would settle the matter.

Surprise.

He slapped the folder shut again. Reaching for the necessary forms, he briskly called out for a runner, and by the time one had been found the warrant requests were ready. While he waited for this business to be done he put out some more requests for files and wrote up the obligatory memorandum to his Captain. Half an hour later, files opened on a desk now cleared of other business, which he had brusquely shifted to his Sergeant and the secretary, Crake was making a series of telephone calls to the City Clerk, the Corporation Commission, the Motor Vehicle Division, and others. At last the warrants came back. He folded them into the long wallet which he used to carry papers, and slipped that, together with the notebook in which he had scribbled the results of his telephone calls, into the inside pocket of his coat.

Getting too warm for a coat, he thought as he stepped out onto Fifth Street. Ten o'clock and temperature in the eighties already. He squinted up at the sky. Cloudless, the sun still below the inverted pyramid of City Hall just up the street.

Crake stopped to look back. One of the palms put in the year before had died, he saw. He thought a dead palm the starkest thing imaginable, nothing but a naked pole topped by a little blackened tuft. A saguaro, picket of naked ribs spearing up from a heap of dried flesh, was too much like common death; and a tree, dead elm or maple, was simply picturesque. Besides which a palm never stood up straight. It never seemed quite to fit into the landscape, and a dead one suggested some Pleistocene devastation of blowing dust and hard sun. Paradise lost.

They never should have put City Hall into that building. It was a satire on government to have the big end up that way. Crake had sometimes had a good harvest of ponegranates from the bushes which grew around the plaza. The last two years, however, had been too hot. No juice. And now another.

As Crake stepped out into the sunlight, prickles ran up his neck and a light film of sweat formed on his scalp. He had five dollars on May 28th as the first day the temperature would break one hundred. That money was as good as lost, it seemed. A fierce summer.

Crossing Fifth at Mill, Crake had a brief apprehension of bad luck, a feeling typically associated with the start of a new case. It passed, as usual. Gas. The limbic brain acting up. Reptile fear of death.

□

Caitlin wondered if Crake had felt any premonition at all.

It was well into spring now, well past the desert rainy season, and the night air warm and dry. Too warm for wine, Caitlin thought, and not warm enough for air conditioning. But no one other than Isela Porres could have told her about those times, about the young Bill Face growing discouraged with the struggle to get a living out of books, about her shy unhappy husband.

James was the utterest child, Isela observed one evening, about all that. He simply believed what he liked, that's all, about the money and the traveling and all. Completely at odds with reality. I suppose I must have been taken in. Else why did I marry him, except for the ride? For the ride.

Yes.

He was always that way, Isela went on, oblivious of the indiscretions of her wine-flushed auditor. Couldn't see his hand in front of his face, James. But I think he knew the truth, anyway. Despite himself, you see. He was such a melancholy man then— I suppose because he knew it wasn't so. Then when Bill pulled back, and the trade went to Woyke's shop, he relaxed quite a bit. He even went a little the other way, cultivated this fustiness a little, you know. It was like him.

When was this?

Bill, of course, wasn't going to simply turn the bookshop over to him. James could be so unrealistic about such things. That was when Bill made his coffee cup a proxy. If James needed Bill's vote he was to ask the cup. I think Bill even wrote it up. I thought it was funny as hell, but James, you know— James was furious. Wouldn't speak for days. Unspeakable. After that he seemed more to know his place. It broke him, Bill's little joke. That was eight, ten years ago. About the time Bill was beginning to invest really heavily in the reconstruction.

He was going places then. James never had any sense of humor. None.

There was a long, ruminating silence. Isela drank half a glass of wine in small sips.

Rufus was such a dear little man about all that. So absurdly stiff, like a penguin, with his short legs. No shoulders at all.

Another long silence, another glass of wine.

I suppose that's why James felt he deserved some consideration later on, you know, when everyone thought he was guilty. Because he had never had any. Silly way of thinking.

Caitlin was astounded. You don't think, she stammered, that he is guilty?

Who?

James. Your husband.

Isela turned distinctly cold, as if she had been caught rambling. Now my dear, she began, what have I been saying? Of course I think so.

Then her voice became uncertain. He was such a tender heart. He couldn't bear it, of course.

Bear what?

Isela laughed, the briefest of cackles.

I understand you've decided to take the bookshop account back?

Caitlin blinked. Again the cackle.

My dear, you must think me quite a fool.

Dominance regained, Isela paused for a sip of wine. But the pause lengthened into a silence, as if she actually expected an answer.

No, Caitlin managed, panicking. No, of course not.

Isela hollered with glee at that, and for the second time Caitlin fled in confusion, making her conventional excuse.

At home, she stripped to a t-shirt and got into bed. Her clothes were left in a pile. She kicked off the bedclothes, too, and turned on the fan.

How easy it is, she thought, for bitter people to be wise.

The fan began to cool her flushed skin. She turned it aside.

The woman treated her as a child. Well, why not? Wasn't she a child?

It would all have to be verified, of course. She wondered
whether there was anything in it at all. Probably not. Is there
anything really true? How easy it must be to be a detective
when everyone is guilty.

Innocence.

The innocence men do lives after.

Make haste to shed innocent blood.

Innocent people, Crake had said once, do a lot of damage.
She'd never been sure what he meant by that.

□

When the forensics men had gone, Crake returned to the store.
Porres, stiffly fixed in position beside the desk, had not moved.
Forensics must have been able to work around him. The body
was gone. Without speaking, Crake stepped briskly to the back
of the store and wiped his hand over the row of three switches
just inside the stockroom door. A weak yellow light washed
over the shelves and was mostly absorbed by the dark brick and
the weathered beams.

Porres cleared his throat. I took out most of the bulbs, he
said apologetically. Bill always liked to have so much light. He
wanted to encourage people to read, you know. But it gave me
headaches, you see. And it's cooler, too, in the dark.

So here the battle was joined, over a petty humiliation. Laurence William Face had been a dominating man.

The ledgers Crake took only because it was always a good
idea to confiscate something. The important accounts were
elsewhere, to be gone over by experts. For half an hour Crake
sat in the only chair, a ring-binder opened under the desk lamp,
casually turning over the ledger pages while Porres waited. Gra-
tuitously, he mixed up the papers on the desk a little. At last
he leaned back in the chair. The atmosphere of the bookshop
irritated Crake. He had never liked this fay redecoration of the
business district. It reminded him of the magazines his wife
used to read—pictures of rooms with no dirt and no kids and
recipes for gourmet picnics. It also made him conscious of
being out of date.

An old building, he thought, ought to look old. Like old skin. As if it had been lived in for a while. He would have liked to pretend that it was traditional honesty that was out of date. But he knew that it was really just that he preferred the lies of his youth. Who wanted to look old?

Crake had made himself angry. Slowly he rose and reached for the stock ladder, leaning nearby, and his arms and shoulders quivered as if he meant to break it in half. But he managed to spread it calmly enough, though he tried to drive the legs through the floor as he set it up beside the desk. Finally he vented his resentment by methodically destroying the primness of the upper shelves, pulling the books down by twos and threes, roughing them up, putting them back upside down, on their fore edges so that the covers splayed out, piled up or jammed in on top of those standing farther down. There was nothing in the books themselves that Bill could have wanted. Perhaps on the shelves behind them.

Here, he muttered, beginning to clear the books away.

Crake, turning with books in each hand to pass down, met the eyes of Porres below. He smiled, feeling again in control. Porres grew pale in turn. They were like two wooden men in a toy barometer, Crake thought, going round and round at opposite ends of the same stick, alternately pink and blue, in and out of a tick-tock house with a false front.

Shelf by shelf revealed nothing but an undisturbed layer of dust until the top one, which Crake had saved for last. Here too, the shelf space behind the books was empty, but the dust was smudged. Crake hunched his shoulders up against the ceiling and thrust his head more into the opening. There were three marks altogether, with a little dust, not more than a day's accumulation, lying over the smudges. Crake gazed at the pattern for some time, meditating, before he stepped down again to the floor. Then, taking his own gun from its holster, he cleared out another shelf of books at a convenient height and carefully laid the revolver in the dust at the back of the shelf. It rested on two points: the cylinders and the lower edge of the grip. After a moment, Crake reached out and picked up the gun with a slight turn of his wrist, a natural scooping motion

that smeared out the mark left by the butt of the gun and cre-
ated a third, a short curved line made by the tip of the barrel.
The three marks corresponded exactly to those on the top shelf.

Crake put his gun away and stood for several moments con-
templating the disordered shelves. Then he walked slowly to
the back of the store, absently taking books from the shelves,
turning over a few pages, and laying them down again somewhere.

The stock room was more to Crake's liking. No effort had
been made to make it presentable: unpainted wooden shelves
were thrown up on two walls to hold inventory and on the floor
was a plain high table for unpacking or preparing shipments,
with dispensers of tape and string, a stack of mailing labels, and
a box knife lying on top. Against the third wall stood a bat-
tered green filing cabinet holding invoices and correspondence.
A supply of flattened boxes was wedged between the file and
the wall and on the other side of the file was a heap of used
padded mailers. A squat old desk of blond wood, with a wooden
caster chair to match, stood farther down beneath a lamp with
a wide metal shade.

Crake rummaged through the desk, which was empty save for
some pencils and a pad of lined yellow paper, and looked into
the files enough to satisfy himself that he could do nothing with
them on his own. The box knife he slipped into his pocket.
There would be blood on it, of course. There was always blood
on a box knife. He scrutinized the floor, which appeared to
have been swept, and the scarred surface of the table, without
success. In a corner between the shelves and the back wall of
the building was a folding cot which Crake took out and set up,
but it had obviously not been used in some time. Finally he
opened the delivery door and stepped out into the alley where
he stood for a long while in the sunshine, looking away toward
the north, at the butte with its glaring letter A. Every town in
the valley was lettered, which he'd found quite odd at first.
Nothing about the desert seemed odd anymore. The letter was
supposed to be white, but was repainted every so often as a
prank. At the moment it was striped red and blue.

In an effort to create off-street parking, reconstruction had opened up the alleys behind Mill Avenue with pocket parks and parking lots. The Avenue would then be widened to six lanes for rush hour traffic, which was always heavy in the winter when the river was running and the unbridged crossings were closed. The back-street parks were good places for folk fairs and craft shows, and several regular events that drew good crowds had grown up in the last ten years. It was good for business. He hated it. In Crake's thirty years a run-down desert town had been turned first into a booming bedroom suburb and then a center of power for the computer industry. There was money everywhere. Air-conditioning half the surface of the earth raised the temperature of the other half ten degrees and universal irrigation doubled the relative humidity. Development had brought all the disadvantages of a city without any of the pleasures which Crake remembered from his Chicago childhood: long summer days riding the buses through strange neighborhoods, a fragrant delicatessen on the corner with glass cases of food with unpronounceable names, piss-stained movie theatres showing everything from twenty years before. Maybe there would be strange neighborhoods here in another thirty years, and things would be fragrant and piss-stained by then, but what good was that to him? If he had wanted only that he could have died where he was, in Chicago.

What had Bill wanted a gun for? Tire marks in the gravel of the parking lot showed that Bill's car had been moved at least once during the night. Had he perhaps been attacked by someone hiding in the bushes? Was it really possible to hide under such bushes? Retreating back inside for the gun, he was followed and killed, and the car borrowed afterward to dispose of evidence. What evidence? And where was the gun now?

Crake shrugged and went back inside. Porres was busily putting the shelves in order, his bald head flushed with exertion and annoyance.

How often do you sweep out, Jim?

Every morning. Porres's voice was a bit thick. Obviously he disliked being called Jim.

When did you get your last shipment, Jim?

Friday afternoon. I opened it this morning.

So you've been industriously at work. Laudable. Didn't cut yourself with the box knife this morning, did you?

Cut myself? No.

Did you know your partner kept a gun in the store?

No. I suppose it was from years ago, when we kept open nights.

Used to sleep in the store, did he?

Sometimes. You mean the cot in the back.

Mmm. So the gun has been up on that shelf five, seven years. Your stock doesn't turn over very fast, does it?

Well, no, I don't suppose it can have been there all the time. Not more than six months, perhaps?

Mm. Know how to shoot? I suppose not.

No.

Let em have the till, is my advice. What was the gun for?

I have no idea.

Porres had sat down at his desk during the course of these preliminary questions. Now Crake sat on the desk itself, crumpling the papers and looming over his slighter adversary, forcing Porres to lean back precariously in his chair in order to meet the hectoring detective's eyes.

Let me see, Jim. You rode to work on your bicycle as usual. Came in the back. Saw nothing. Opened the mail lying on the work table, carried it in to your desk and found the evil thing lying on the floor just here. Eh?

Yes.

Didn't notice Willy's fancy car parked outside, I suppose?

Certainly I did.

Didn't give it a thought.

Actually not. Bill used to leave his car there sometimes. If he had been making the rounds of the bars and was unable to drive. If he had gone home with someone else.

Mm, said Crake, continuing. Now let's see. If Billyum's neck was broken by a stranger then it must have been on the spot, look you, because unless he was caught reaching for the gun a stranger wouldn't have known it was there. And it would still be there, whereas if he had actually succeeded in getting it down then we would see some sign of an unarmed man's scrambling out of the way, which we do not. Eh?

Yes.

And where has the gun toddled off to? Eh?

Why do you think Bill was murdered?

Just so. And none of this explains, does it, what he was doing here? In the middle of the night?

He'd caught a burglar.

Ah, yes. A burglar who was rifling the desk, here, and failed to notice Billyum creep past, set up the ladder, and crawl up for his gun.

Porres set his jaw and looked down at his hands.

Perhaps Willie brought the trouble in with him, Crake went on. Someone not so savory. Know anyone like that? Any of Willie's midnight friends?

No.

Thought not. A little chippie, perhaps.

Porres started. After a moment he began slowly to flush red, like grenadine in a tequila sunrise.

Well, continued Crake, after observing this with interest, but this line of thinking makes it a bit harder to explain the gun, doesn't it. Picked himself up one of those women, I suppose, who can't get off without the fear of death to loosen them up. A little discussion with a business associate, perhaps, and the talk turned acrimonious. A blackmailer. Billy leave any secrets in your keeping?

No.

Thought not. An arsonist, then, previously in Billy's employ. A necessary working tool for a real estate developer, of course, at least in the old country. Good way to get started. Not so good later on.

We've had no fires.

Yes, we've been lucky that way, haven't we? We'll stick to the fires of passion. An outraged father, shall we say, or a poor husband maddened by the sight of cold metal in the little woman's quim?

Porres made a swallowed protest, but Crake only bore down harder. As he shifted his weight, some crumpled pamphlets slid off onto the floor.

Now your stock ladder, I notice, has a loose step. Maybe we

can come up with something a little simpler, Jim. Willbert loses
his balance and breaks his neck. A clean job. Whoever blew in
with him takes the gun, which would raise a few eyebrows, and
just for good measure washes up the coffee cup. You noticed
that, I imagine? A lot to be explained yet in that one, but I'm
sure we can come up with something plausible. We always do.

Porres had finally begun to squirm. Why was there necessar-
ily another person here? he objected. His voice had gone tight.

Ah. Billie takes away the gun a week or so ago, is that it?
Then on Wednesday night he comes in by himself, falls down
and dies.

Yes.

The coffee cup is a bit of a problem, Jim. Not an insoluble
problem, perhaps. Washed it himself. Then there's the books.
Someone put them all back on the shelf. I'm sure you noticed
that, Jim. Standing a little crooked, no dust on em? You're a
neat man, Jim. Local wino, maybe. Finds the back door hanging open and comes in to get warm, spots the corpse, barks his
shin on the desk in a hurry to get out.

In fact, there was a bruise visible on Porres's leg. Perspiration
was beginning to dampen his shirt now and Crake paused, spec-
ulating.

In pretty good shape are you, Jim?

Good enough, I suppose.

How far do you ride from home?

Three miles. Three and a quarter.

Hardly enough to work up a sweat, eh?

They had reached the twitching stage. Porres still kept himself under control, however, and said nothing.

Whoever was here, Crake went on, a bit more quietly now
that his points were beginning to be felt, cautiously so as not to
release the sufferer by accident. Whoever was here knew of or
was able to discover the existence of Bill's revolver, else we will
have to explain why Bill was up on the ladder. Whoever was
here touched up the scene to make it look a little more accidental. The coroner will be able to tell us if the body was moved,
of course. I don't think it was, myself.

Closing his eyes, Porres began to sag. Crake had never met

anyone able to stand up to this sort of interrogation. The more blameless they were the faster they wilted. A completely blameless person, he supposed, would wilt instantly. There didn't seem, however, to be any such. Crake finished the recital.

And whoever else was here, Jim, had a key to the shop.

Porres jerked upright. Crake laughed.

The place was locked up, Jim. You unlocked it yourself this morning. You haven't told me a little fib?

No. It was locked.

Yes. Well, the second person locked up as he left, because if Bill had come in alone he would have locked the door behind him and that's the way it had to appear. Bill's own key was still in his pocket. The other person, then, had a key of his own. How many keys are there, Jim?

As Porres seemed unable to reply, Crake answered himself.

Bill's. Yours, with which you opened up the next morning. And one for Caitlin Vachon. Three.

Porres choked, like a flooded engine, and came to life at last. But under Crake's cynical appraisal he quickly died, and Crake chuckled quietly.

It would look much better, Jim, if you had spoken up a little earlier, at the part about outraged husbands. Ah well. Let me have a squint at your key, eh?

Porres fumbled in his pocket and brought out a chain, which he dropped into the detective's hand. Crake separated the right key from the rest and returned the chain.

Tch, he said, squinting at the key.

Porres found his voice finally. These innuendos are ridiculous, he sputtered. You could suspect me as well as anyone.

Oh, I do, Crake replied lightly. I do, Jim.

He laid the key gently on the desk between them.

□

Caitlin got into her car but did not start the engine. Instead, she leaned against the door, resting the back of her neck on the open window, and stared up into the warm moonless sky. So the question of what Bill had been doing in the store in the mid-

dle of the night seemed to be answered, at least: sticking his
hand in the till. Who knew about that? Everyone, apparently.
Chagrined, Caitlin tried to blink away the memory of Isela's
laughter.

It did suggest some new lines, however. Suppose Bill had
been surprised in the course of one of these raids? A burglar,
surprised. His partner, lying in wait against him. An argument.
A scramble for the gun. So innocuous.

There was always the possibility that Bill was murdered somewhere else, that the body was carried in and the whole scene
manufactured from scratch by someone who knew Bill's habit,
knew about the gun, knew that just such an explanation would
suggest itself because everyone, after all, knew. Why hadn't it
suggested itself, then?

So complicated. Instinctively, Caitlin did not believe in complicated explanations in the same way that she did not believe
in evil, or in compliments. The world is simple and elegant, was
her view, and appearances to the contrary were just that, and
people who thought otherwise thought so because they were
not in possession of the facts.

It was true, she wasn't in possession of the facts. Had Crake
known? Why had he been so secretive, so that now it was necessary to begin again? Surely he had come at least this far. Yet
Isela claimed never to have seen the detective.

And what about the coffee cup? If she were to create an
accident from scratch would she leave the coffee cup clean or
not?

Was one ever actually in possession of the facts? Was it even
a good idea to be in possession? Then she reconsidered. What
nonsense: ineffable facts.

Milo Crake had been an old hand, hadn't he? In a moment
he decided the case, handily: a murder, and James Porres somehow responsible. Wasn't that just what being an old hand
meant, to not be put off by the facts? No understanding without abstraction, no truth without lies.

Caitlin sat up, dug her keys out of her purse, and started the
engine. As she pulled out into the street, out of the shelter of
the building, a hot wind shook the car, a damp thick wind laden

with dust and the smell of rain. It was not rain, but only the
irrigation, the weekly night-time release of water. It wouldn't
rain for weeks yet. Not until August.

□

James Porres was bent over his desk when Crake entered. A bell
attached to the door jangled persistently as Crake paused in the
doorway to wait for his eyes to adjust. Did the man do nothing
but pore over catalogs in the dark? There was something irritating to Crake about people who work in the dark. The bell's
tiny piercing note sounded again and again. At last Porres
raised his head.

Good morning.

As if Crake were another customer for the works of Robert
Musil or Eugene Sue. And perhaps he was, to this foolishly
saintly antiquarian, unless he insisted otherwise.

You remember me, I think. Lieutenant Milo Crake.

Oh yes, of course I do.

Crake stepped forward into the light cast by the desk lamp at
Porres's elbow.

I have a warrant, he said, extracting the paper from his
wallet.

Porres started. What for?

Crake unfolded the warrant and laid it on the desk where,
like a night-blooming flower, it slowly folded itself up again.

Why, for your arrest, James, if I should need it.

If you were able to get a warrant, Porres observed quietly,
then you must have some suspicion of murder.

Crake pursed his lips, inclined his head, smiled.

Porres laid down his pencil. I thought, he said, it was clear
that Bill fell from the stock ladder and struck his head. Here.

He rose somewhat in his chair and put his finger on the spot,
directly under the lamplight, as if he were moving his man on a
chessboard. His fingers were stubby, flat, badly manicured.

That may be, Crake replied. If so, he didn't die from that.

Eh? Porres seemed genuinely puzzled, like a dog when one
only pretends to throw the stick.

The blood on the desk was not Bill's, it seems. Also, it was fresher by several hours than the blood in the wound.

Porres collapsed into his chair. There was a long silence.

Then what did he die of?

Oh, broke his neck, indubitably.

So he did fall from the stock ladder?

Well, that's a bit hasty. But he does seem to have bonked himself on the corner of the desk somehow. Little spot on the back of his head, you remember. Crake indicated the place, on the crest of bone behind his ear. Doesn't seem as if the body was moved, so the desk is a likely item.

So it was an accident after all.

James, James. Little tiff, boy hops up on the ladder to get his gun. Kick the ladder out from under, he falls and breaks his neck.

Why should I do that?

Ah.

The two men's eyes met in lengthening silence.

Yes, said Crake at last. That's the nubbin, isn't it? The cookie.

Silence.

Tough little bugger when it comes down to it.

I think, Jim, we'd better have you over for an official chat. You want to call your wife and tell her not to wait supper?

□

Much of what Crake found out later came from Woyke's shop boy Luther Idge, that was clear. Caitlin thought perhaps she too ought to do a little more in that direction.

After Woyke's departure, Porres had taken over the store across the street but had so far left the management of it to Idge, and it was there that she found him. Yes, the store was doing well. Better, actually, than what Woyke had done.

Luther waved a deprecating hand, not wanting to disparage his old employer. It was the recession, he said. Hard times are always good for the book business.

Why is that?

Cheap entertainment. Travel to exotic places.

He picked a book from a rack nearby, a recent novel about, Caitlin read from the jacket liner, the last white emperor of a now-forgotten black empire.

Luther shrugged. The novel as anthropology, eh? The last refuge of the story-teller. Costs more'n a movie, but it lasts longer and there's no babysitter needed. Goes down easy.

Caitlin returned the book with annoyance. So many worldly people all of a sudden. Luther's happy vision of himself as a pander seemed accurate enough.

What can I do for you? he asked, and went volubly on without waiting for an answer. Mr. Porres is doing pretty well, too, isn't he? All you need is a little opportunity to show what you can do. Bill Face kept people down. Mr. Woyke complained about it.

At this opportune moment the telephone rang. Luther answered brightly, scurried to the shelves to check his stock for the caller, and came back empty-handed. A slightly ill-natured haggling over prepayment of a special order ensued, and meanwhile Caitlin explored the shop.

Idge had removed all trace of Woyke's genteel humanism. She thought the stock had lost character: the serious books were gone from history and psychology; philosophy had been transformed into religion; the ubiquitous distinction between fiction and literature had been put into place and the serious novels moved to the back. The children's books were gone, and there was no science with numbers in it. At the same time, all the frivolous books were gone, too. Woyke had had a few hobbyhorses. The new shop was a place to go on a lunch hour run for a package of pantyhose. It was too safe to last very long, she thought.

How many hours do you put in here? she asked, returning to the counter. Luther was sweating over an order form, grumbling to himself.

Seventy or eighty.

No help?

Luther's attention was now on the little CRT hidden under the lip of the counter. He pressed this button and that. Satisfied finally, he entered the record with a little flourish and looked up.

I can't afford help, he said. There's only one living in a bookshop.

Woyke had help.

The help didn't make a living, either.

I thought you said business was up.

It's up, Luther returned impatiently, his uncertain command of the salesman's bonhomie slipping a little. Mr. Woyke wouldn't peddle the right stuff. He got by on handouts and cheap help.

Handouts?

Well, not to notice. Rent kept low, a few big tabs picked up by the parent company, that sort of thing.

The parent being one of Bill's real estate outfits?

I guess, said Luther blandly. Mr. Woyke, you know, knew just what he had, just what would move, just what he had to move to get by. But he wouldn't move it. He wanted to sell this other stuff. Missionary stuff. Bill Face kept him on credit anyway. Two alike, but Bill got by with it somehow.

Mr. Porres would give you credit, do you think?

Luther smiled. I'm on my own, he said. It's good business.

Bill Face got a living plus enough to get started out of the book business, Caitlin observed, with just a touch of maliciousness. How did he do that?

Yes, I'll tell you how he did that.

Caitlin was looking at the knot of Luther's tie, a strangled sort of knot which had been pulled to one side, under the parsimonious collar, exposing the button.

I'll tell you how he managed, Luther said, reddening with anger. He put in a hundred hours a week, not sixty. He peddled books, shook hands, dunned accounts, wheedled bankers and salesmen, dodged collection agents, arranged readings, wrote copy, cadged, talked, pushed. Always talking, always pushing. Every spare nickel came out. He lived in a garbage dump with a rusted-out swamp cooler and ate crackers for supper and wore shirts without backs. You call that a living?

Taken aback, Caitlin was unable to reply.

And Porres stuck it, waited twenty years for his own, might have waited twenty more except for a lucky accident. I'm surprised his wife didn't tell him to piss off earlier. Stupid bugger.

Again a grating silence, which Caitlin didn't know how to break. At last Luther awakened. He smiled sourly and apologized.

Well, business is up, but I'm getting out. What can I do for you? he asked, beginning over.

Actually, you've already told me a good deal of what I wanted to know.

Luther gave a single bark of laughter. So you're mucking about in the Face murder? You'll regret it.

Apparently.

Things lie as well as they will. It's no business of yours, is it?

You know a good deal about it.

I don't know anything about it. Why do you think you can find out something the police couldn't? You couldn't even find out my mother's name. You'll stir things up, make all the wrong people mad, and only end up offending your own sense of justice.

Who do you think was in it, then?

What do you care? Are you one of these vigilantes who worry about what other people's kids read? I get one of them a week, at least. What have I got in here, for god's sake? Huckleberry Finn. If I sold only the straight stuff I'd go hungry. Don't buy it if you don't think you'll like it.

Bad for business.

No bricks yet. Sure I think Mr. Woyke was responsible. He was a very responsible person. You know when I was a kid I sprayed DDT on my cat? That was back when people left DDT laying around, you know. I had an idea it was flea powder. The cat had fleas so bad its fur was coming out. Killed the fleas too, I guess. My mom told me the cat ran away, but I figured it out for myself after a while.

Luther stared vacantly off toward the back of the store for a time. At last he sighed and pulled himself together a bit.

You know, he said, I think the cops missed one thing. They worked over this poor sod of Soccorro's, you know, the one whose Volkswagen she used to off herself. Well, he didn't know anything, of course. He'd only just picked her up. Then who's the guy we see her with around here all the time? You ought to talk to that one. The cops didn't pick up on that, I think. They assumed there was only one guy in it.

It sounds as if she got around a little.

A little, I guess. Anything with less than six legs, anyway. She and Bill would have made a good pair. To bad it didn't last.

Why didn't it?

Well, he died, didn't he?

Slipped out of a sticky spot, eh?

That's it.

You don't look old enough to remember DDT.

Luther looked bluntly at her, startled, and then grinned widely. You're all right, he said. Come up and see me some time.

Sure.

Come on. Why are you in this?

I don't know, she said, as honestly as she could.

Do you always muck around in other people's business that way? Without knowing what you're doing?

Never.

I believe it. There's a pot of gold nobody's found yet, I can tell you. That Bill Face was no monkey. But I guess you know that.

He smiled, appraising her.

Come round after work. We'll have drinks.

Sure.

There were only a few minutes left in her lunch hour. Caitlin bought a tuna sandwich and a cookie at a shop up the street and slipped into one of the shaded courtyards to wolf it down. Now, at the height of summer, half the shops were closed and the courtyard was empty. The paloverde which shaded her bench rattled softly in a fitful breeze. A little soft jazz was coming from the open back door of a shop selling used records. Caitlin took a deep breath to stop the pounding flow of blood in the pit of her stomach before she began to eat.

What an aggravating little man. She thought he was hardly older than twenty-five. What did he have to be so cynical about?

But Luther Idge had been right about Bill: Caitlin remembered him talking about late nights, eighteen-hour days, camping in the back of the shop and living for a week on a box of crackers. They had been his best memories, too. That was something he had done just for himself, while his body was still strong enough, before he had thought of power, before ambition had made him finicky.

James Porres's strength, discovered so late, was going to be a different thing, she suspected. It came from pride. He would never be able to see a defeat as an inconvenience, a bore, a chance to unload a liability. Rather it was a strike at his soul, potentially fatal. Late success, she thought, was probably mostly ashes.

She had been fond of James Porres once, and he had seemed interested enough in her. Once, she hadn't disliked him. Not until circumstances had pushed him forward. He had been a nice enough man. Eccentric, inclined to whimsies and a little harmless testiness, luxuries of character cultivated in the leisure which Bill provided him.

It was Bill who held them all together—his women, his friends, his contacts, the crowd of proteges and retainers with which he surrounded himself, the groupie fringe. He lent himself to them all, by a system of bookkeeping which emphasized cash flow over striking balances.

Keep moving, he said. You'll be all right.

But he had lost his balance after all.

Things came apart after that. It had been a one-man empire. The parts hadn't belonged together, they'd only stuck together for him. If Porres succeeded in pulling any of it back together it would be on a much smaller scale and in a different style. No credit. You wouldn't be in it for him, but for yourself.

Crake's instincts had been good. He hadn't bothered about the body, or explaining the evidence, or any of that. He had looked straight through all of them. You, he said. You're responsible. You did this somehow. It's your fault.

Well really, what else could he do? What did the evidence come to, after all?

She finished the sandwich and rolled the plastic in which it

had been wrapped into a little ball. Slowly, obstinately, it flattened itself out again.

Caitlin was late for work. She went back out onto the street,
drawing the big brim of her straw hat down over her face as she
passed into the sunlight. The temperature sign at the end of the
block stood at 116 degrees.

She minded the heat. Bill hadn't.

Bill Face had had quite unusual talents. When he died no one
cared particularly. Except herself. But if it had been James
Porres who had lost his balance it would have been just the
same, a little clucking of tongues and then silence. Wasn't there
something wrong with that? Two so very different men?

When her mind returned to the problem at hand, Caitlin forgot all about the disagreeable Luther Idge and the chain of
reflections he had provoked. Find Soccorro's gigolo, had been
his advice. Disagreeable or not, he was right. That had been
overlooked.

But who was he? Seen and yet never seen: a middle-aged
man with a gray moustache and a gray car. The sort of man
who doesn't own a knit shirt. Nothing else.

Well, Soccorro would have had to meet him somewhere. For
several nights running, Caitlin made the rounds of likely bars.
Plenty of people remembered Soccorro Porres. Some of them
remembered a man with a gray moustache and a three-piece
suit, too, when she suggested it. But the truth seemed to be
that Soccorro had been the sort of girl who is seen with everyone. Caitlin drank too much, said no too much, and that was
that. Luther Idge was right about another thing: she wasn't
able to find out her own name without asking her mother.

□

One day toward the end of August Caitlin realized that she had
not thought about Bill Face's death in some time. She hadn't
thought about him at all. For the first time in five years he was
not somewhere in her thoughts. The little underwater cave
where he had lurked was empty. It was a relief, actually.

Walking up Mill Avenue after lunch she counted up and discovered that it had actually been only four months since Bill's death. It had seemed much longer. But then the summers always seemed long. It was the heat.

The Mill Avenue Title Company was closed. A scrawled sign standing on the window ledge gave James Porres's home telephone number. A second sign, taped to the window, gave the realtor's name and number. Four hundred twenty square feet, the sign said. That little? Peering through the dusty window, Caitlin could see about halfway back into the darkness. Everything was gone. There was a pencil lying on the floor near the door.

After lunch she called the number listed as Porres's and got a recorded message. Mr. Porres has stepped out and will return shortly, said an unfamiliar woman's voice. If you will leave your name and number, and state the nature of your business, he will endeavor to return your call.

This was followed by a beep and a hissing silence. Caitlin mulled over the nature of her business until at last the line went dead and she left it just as it was, a puka.

She called the telephone company. There was no listing for James, James A., or J.A. Porres. The number listed in the city directory for the house on Greenway Drive had been disconnected. The number given on the sign in the shop was for a rundown old house on Ash, two blocks away, but when she went around there after work it was vacant.

She called the realtor. As she had expected, the rent was a bit high. But yes, it was a prime location. She stopped by City Hall to look at the tax rolls and the next morning she called the Recorder. Bank business, she said. Ordinary callers did not get reference service.

The house on Greenway Drive, two hundred thousand inches from work, was in the hands of the same agency that was renting the store, prime business location and all, for too much money. It was one of Bill's old companies, part of an entity once called Mill Enterprises, which had been incorporated at the beginning of August as Mill Associates, papers signed by a woman whose name was unfamiliar to Caitlin until she found it again as the owner of the house on Ash.

So James was on his way.
Caitlin waved. Goodbye, goodbye.

□

Isela Porres had no need to wait supper; she never cooked anything to begin with. She had never in her life, it seemed to her,
had a proper family supper. Her father had worked in a copper
mine while she was growing up—the swing shift, to avoid them—
the children. There were too many of them, and Isela's mother
had not managed well. One of Isela's first memories was of sitting dumbly in her high chair waiting to be cleaned after upset-
ting a bowl of milk-soaked farina, while her oldest sister, half
made up, stood in her underwear beside the open refrigerator,
looking on, eating cottage cheese from the box. It was winter.
A pot of something which had burned on the stove had been
standing in the sink for days, and the air was thick with smudge
and smelter fumes. The back door stood open, admitting a
chill evening breeze, and there her mother stood, cheek pressed
to the jamb. Isela remembered every detail of their back lot,
seen through the torn screen on that day at sunset: the scattered tufts of dormant brown grass, the ochre dirt washed pink
in the weak light and spangled here and there by salty white
outcrops of caliche, the back fence of prickly pear. One of the
cactus pads was broken half off and hung, a single fruit clinging
to its edge so red, passionate.

Isela remembered eating cactus pads. Nopales, a traditional
Mexican dish. But who had cooked them? One of her sisters?
She was the youngest. Her mother would have been in her early
forties at the time, a little older than Isela was now. Isela had
confined herself to one child.

Her husband was always late. In twenty years in the book
business he had never been home before six-thirty. When Soccorro was small Isela had fed her separately, at five o'clock.
Now Soccorro looked after herself. Isela and James ate later,
when they ate together. Isela watched with despair her ado-

49

lescent daughter, half made up, in her underwear, go to the refrigerator for a box of cottage cheese.

Isela always wanted to have a formal supper, with table fully laid, cloth napkins, wine, separate plates for salad. For years, nearly all her adult life, she had insisted without success on this dignity. Then she stopped insisting.

Three days a week she worked for a florist, assembling corsages, funeral wreaths, and tacky little things with plastic animals and baby's breath. When she came home on Monday night there was nothing to eat but the cottage cheese and a frozen pizza. She broke off a piece of pizza for herself and put it into the microwave oven, but before she could turn on the oven the telephone rang.

The five-thirty salesman, a regular nuisance call. Since James began to ride a bicycle to work this had become a thing of small anxiety. What if he had been run over?

The caller had a disagreeable, harsh voice. He claimed to be an attorney, a Mr. Whizzer of the firm of Whing and Scissors, or something to that effect. Her husband, it seemed, had been detained for questioning in the murder of Laurence Face and would not be home on time. Attorney Whizzer then hung up.

Isela blinked. What on earth? Surely the man's name couldn't have been Whizzer. What had happened to Phillips, who had always advised them? Laurence Face? She hadn't heard him called Laurence in years, not since that black poet. The woman wanted to marry him; she'd given him money, obscene little thingamabobs that were supposed to be key chains or letter openers, rubbed him up, cursed him on the street—

Arrested? What?

Your father won't be home for a while, she said when Soccorro came down a few minutes later. He's been arrested.

What? Soccorro was brushing her hair and seemed not to have heard.

For murdering Bill Face.

What?

Isela watched in vain for understanding in her daughter. I suppose, she said after a considerable pause, thoughtfully, this means we won't be going to Michigan again this year.

Soccorro was at last aware of what her mother was saying:
that her father would be late, so late that he was not coming
home again. She stopped brushing her hair.

Bill was murdered?

So they say.

On the phone?

Yes. A lawyer. He assumed I knew all about it. In the murder of Laurence Face.

Laurence?

The point of Soccorro's tongue emerged and circled her lips
slowly. Soccorro, in shorts and halter, with that line of black
hair which ran down between her breasts to plunge into the
lake below, and her tongue, like a fish—

Isela felt the blood come to her face and drops of sweat form
in her armpits.

The hairline covered the seam where the mold separated, at
least.

Color drained from the world, pressed out of it by the explosion of a headache that pushed her eyes from their sockets.
Isela whimpered, one soft note which escaped her self-control
before the moment was over.

Well I suppose, Soccorro observed, that if he's murdered they
would want to talk to Father about it.

Her mother's freezing stare told her new things about adult
passions, their perversity and depth.

The evening passed slowly. Isela fell asleep as if electrocuted,
upstairs, with her clothes on. Soccorro sat in the darkening
kitchen with a glass of milk.

They had taken him up for questioning. Well, they would.
Soccorro had never seen the city jail, did not know where it
was. She had never seen the police station, either, or been ques-
tioned by the police aside from what she got from running a
stop sign a month after earning her license. She saw her bald,
timid father there, in jail, and was horrified by the care which
her imagination lavished on details: the nails of the man who
took fingerprints, the smell of the successive corridors and
rooms, the soft paper forms which adhered slightly to each
other and would not make a neat pile, and the obsessive way in

which the inspector marched half a dozen rubber stamps back
and forth across his desk all during the questioning.

State your name.

James Frederick Porres.

Age and occupation.

I am forty-four, a bookseller.

Lieutenant Crake, content to observe, had taken a seat against
the wall. Porres and his examiner sat at a small rosewood conference table, the center of light, while the rest of the room
remained dim. The drapes which covered one wall were closed
—drapes of some dark color, lined to keep out the sun and the
heat. Along the wall opposite the window ran a bank of black
lateral files and in front of the files a walnut desk faced the covered window. The conference table had been placed behind the
door so that a clerk, receiving instructions from Crake in the
open doorway, could see nothing of who was being interro-
gated. Porres was kept from casual scrutiny. The examiner
made every effort to appear calm. He stretched long legs out
over the chocolate carpet, crossed them, gazed at the instep of
one pallid snakeskin boot. With a finger he fished in the pocket
of his vest for a paper clip. Pushing his glasses back slightly,
shrugging the heavy lenses up with a quick facial movement,
brushing some dust from his dark coat, adjusting again the
folder of papers on the table, he began the questioning.

We will pass over, for the time being, the details of your family and business, the inadequacies of your character, your
accumulated sins, and so forth. For the moment, we are interested in your relations with Laurence William Face, with whom
you were acquainted for something more than twenty years, I
believe.

Yes.

The interrogator smiled faintly and began to straighten out
the paper clip he had found in his pocket.

Your relations with the deceased were not entirely smooth.
You had little in common . . .

So it went, hour after hour: the thin elegance of the inquisitor, and Porres: upright, small, pale. Twice the door was
opened: once when coffee and hamburgers were brought in and

then much later, by someone who asked for Lieutenant Crake in a low voice, urgently. Crake went out into the hall. In a moment he returned, and the interrogation resumed.

Porres was shown a long typewritten list of women's names, raggedly aligned, hurriedly prepared. Yes, of course he recognized them—this one, and this, and she, and perhaps others except that he had never learned their names. Caitlin Vachon, certainly. His own wife, Isela. He laid the paper down and returned his hands to his lap.

Well, yes. And if she had? Couldn't he forgive it?

There was a second sheet of paper, as badly typed, bearing the names of men. Business acquaintances: bankers, lawyers, accountants, realtors, the tenants of shops. Porres knew them all. He put his finger down in several places on the list. Here, and here, this one—tiredly. These especially.

And your own business relationships, Mr. Porres?

Good enough. He and Bill had made their start together. Afterward, when Bill no longer took such an interest in the store, he continued to come by nevertheless.

Did you see each other socially?

No, not for many years. They would have embarrassed each other, would they not?

Have you never thought of buying out the partnership?

Yes, several times.

And with what result?

None. He doubted whether Bill would have consented.

Surprised, the inquisitor bent forward and gazed at Porres with cool interest.

Oh, it was a pumpkin, Porres assured him. The whole empire, made from a pumpkin. An illusion. He dasn't sell the pumpkin.

The inquisitor leaned back again, steepling his fingers. The faint scratching of Crake's pen stopped, went on, stopped again.

Yes, I think I understand that. The light glinted from his gray lenses as he inclined his head, began fishing in his pocket for a new paper clip.

And what of this Rufus Woyke?

A tenant.

Didn't Mr. Face consider it poor business to give space to a competitor?

Mr. Face's ideas of business were not the usual.

How long has Mr. Woyke been in business?

Three years.

Yes, thirty-eight months, I believe. He is successful?

Apparently not.

No? Why?

He couldn't say. Once, Porres himself had made a living out of the trade. Perhaps things had changed since then. Perhaps one could not move trade books in that quantity any longer.

Trade?

New books, from commercial publishers.

Ah. Mr. Woyke was a liability, then, but Face continued to carry him. Why?

Did he. Of course there was no reason for Porres to have known that. Sentiment, perhaps.

Ah. Now if you will turn your attention to this matter of—

And so they went over the same ground again and again. Here he had slipped a bit from the truth, here misrepresented a small point. Here he had escaped serious temptation only to fall a little farther on, to stumble there—

Caitlin was conscious of doing all this over, of Lieutenant Crake's presence, of his square back blocking the view. She wasn't certain where he had been, or what conclusion he had reached. All she really knew was why he had so badly wanted to convict James Porres, why he had allowed it to possess him so completely. She too wanted to be scoured clean by desert sand, wanted the clear desert light, wanted to be dried and tough. The Face murder was nothing of the sort.

Lieutenant Crake was like a dead cat lying on the sidewalk, blocking the way to work. And Soccorro Porres also, crushed in the wreckage of that stolen red Volkswagen, already rotting. And there were other things which Caitlin was afraid to look at too closely: the child caught up too soon in adult passions, the consumptive love, the first struggles against knowledge: that you are your parent's child, that you are falling to earth, that

you will do nothing. Caitlin would not for years be able to face
such memories. Would she ever? Crake had been struggling yet
at the end.

The search for reasons would always make her hungry, it
seemed, like the woman in the nursery rhyme: the more she ate
the less she weighed, until finally she vanished.

She had never loved Bill, despite what Isela thought. Yet in a
way she had, and Crake sniffed that out, smelling it like a dog
the odor of her blood.

It was really not so long ago, five years. That was less than
twenty percent of her life. Not enough time to have acquired
the antique fondness one feels for a father long buried. Bill had
been forty. Why don't all women burn up their youth on old
men, as she had? She didn't know. But who would want to
grow up slowly? Other than old people, that is.

What do I know? That's the right answer to everything.
That, and maybe.

□

Soccorro's affair with Bill had started in September. Caitlin had
an idea such things always start in the fall, if they're serious.
It's the school rhythm. Knowledge is an autumn thing.

She had known him all her life. He was her godfather, after
all. Her mother's lover all these years. But toward the end of
the summer something happened to her, and all of that didn't
matter. It was the heat, perhaps. Five months of the desert
heat. Heated.

Bill's bedroom window was open. A hot night wind restlessly turned the pages of a magazine lying on the bedside table.
He was thinking of going out for a run. He wanted to sweat, to
leach himself.

It was a long time since he had had to do with anyone so
young. He didn't care for it anymore. The clumsiness, the fra-
gility. He didn't want to go through all that again.

He turned over in bed and touched her stomach. She was
steaming. He burrowed back into the ooze.

She couldn't stop. There was a fatalism in it, an addiction.

She had to have it—the rush, the nod. She panicked. Was her
mother that way too? It made her faint, a little nauseous feeling in the pit of her stomach. Sexual panic.

He never took her out. Where was there to go that would not
end everything? She called him on the telephone, kept him on
the phone for hours.

I want to come up, Bill.

No.

I want to. I have to.

There's someone here. I have guests.

Her voice came back to her with the slight reverberation it
had when he used the remote speaker. She could hear the tin-
kling of glasses, and voices like surf. Where was he? In the bedroom, down under the pile of coats. In his pajamas, awash in
the cool perfume of strangers. Too warm still for coats. The
remote speaker? He was having someone. She began to sweat.

When are they leaving? I'll come up when they're gone.

I'm going out.

You're going to pick someone up.

No.

You are. I've seen you.

There was no reply. She didn't care who was listening.

Bill. I'm lonesome. Please.

He should have learned how to deal with this by now. It was
so common. But he had never mastered the right note of cold-
ness, that paralyzed without killing. It had always been easier
just to gas them. He was not ruthless enough with himself.

The phone was suddenly muffled. Maybe he had stuffed it
under the mattress, or the rug.

She threatened him. She would tattoo his name on her lip.
She would stuff the telephone into her quim, right there in the
parking lot.

Aaanh! She moaned and shrieked. Say something, Bill. Say
something inside me.

Damn. All right. Not before eleven. Park in the garage. I'll
leave the door open. Be sure you close it.

Her money fell down the throat of the telephone. Shaking,
she took a deep breath and slumped against the wall of the

booth, laid her cheek against the glass.

A boy in a sleeveless t-shirt came out of the U-Totem where she had stopped to phone. He was scratching off a lottery ticket, which he now threw down on the parking lot. Their eyes met, held too long. Suddenly afraid, she wrenched open the door of the phone booth, scowled, and got into her car. She couldn't find her keys. The boy shrugged and drove off.

Three hours yet. She stared into the market, watched the clerk stocking cigarettes in the greenish light. A bicycle was lying on the sidewalk in front of her car, thrown down by a kid who was inside playing video games.

It wasn't true that she had seen Bill make a pickup. She supposed he did. She had seen him in bars with women, foxy women with a taste for money. Sometimes she wondered what happened to all those women. Lawyers and baseball players get them. There aren't that many lawyers and baseball players in the world.

Probably it was like anything else. In some parts of the country they make computers, or pig iron, and ship it off to somewhere else where they make artichokes, or foxy women. After a few years no one notices anymore where things come from, or whether they're out of season.

When she was sixteen she had gotten a second driver's license, using an older friend's identification, so that she could go pubcrawling. That was how she first met Bill Face, in the jazz clubs and singles bars. He hadn't known her. That didn't seem so odd, after she thought about it. She never went to the bookstore, after all, and how could he come to the house, because of Isela? He hadn't seen her since she was a baby. Perhaps he hadn't wanted to recognize her. If he did, then he would have to give her up, wouldn't he? It gave him an upset stomach to think about giving her up. He had never been able to give up anyone.

Bill Face stood in an upper window with a cup of coffee, looking out over the night city. The desert lights, strings of the most wonderful amber color, sparkled as they did nowhere else in the world. Below, on the sides of the mountain to which Bill's house clung, festoons of glittering amber beads cascaded

down into the valley, and four lines of them stretched away to
the east, coming to a stop at the foot of a butte almost invisible
in the dark. The crest of the butte stood out dimly against the
deep violet glow of the night sky. Beyond lay the reservation:
cotton fields, bolls full now in November, tiny pallid faces in
the dark, the blackness of the open desert, faces turned to the
sky and the vast desert-dust of stars.

Soccorro's car turned into the driveway and coasted, lights
out and engine off, into the garage. He heard the garage door
come down, the door at the bottom of the stairs open. She
came up in the dark, into the dark bedroom, silently. He
smelled her, put his coffee cup down on the sill, turned.

Who was here tonight? Earlier.

She rolled over and began to run her fingers through the mat
of hair on his chest. He was beginning to turn gray there. The
gray hairs were stiffer than the others.

Business. He stretched out a hand for the cup of cold coffee
standing on the windowsill.

She had seen them: a young Chicano, thin, not very tall, well-
dressed, and a copper-haired woman in dark slacks and a sleeveless white blouse open to the waist.

I know him, I think, she said. Vice squad?

He laughed with surprise.

Mmm. Do you pay them off?

Bill got up on one elbow and looked at her—her loose hair on
the pillow, mischievous eyes, hands folded easily on her stomach.

No.

Bullshit.

He shrugged and collapsed again, set the empty cup on the
rug beside the bed.

This is not a fast town, he said. There's money, but not fast
money. These are not the guys with the diamond rings and the
big cars. What we have here are television announcers with
wigs, fat company presidents whose idea of a good time is
thirty-six holes of golf instead of eighteen, or drinks and a quick
one over lunch. Doctors' widows with blue hair and thick port-
folios. The big money here is in dull things like real estate, in-

surance. Computers. Not whole computers, mind you. Micro-processors: middle-aged women in white coats and hairnets sitting at microscopes with tweezers. The stink of ozone everywhere.

Who was the woman?

Bill smiled, amused to find himself so fiercely cross-examined by a child.

Some chippie he picked up for you to skin, I suppose. Did he get to watch?

No. You're jealous.

Yes.

Are you jealous of your mother?

No. Did I embarrass you when I called?

Yes. Why did you want to embarrass me?

I had to see you. I couldn't stand it. I was lonesome.

You won't let go.

You should have told me you were a white slaver.

You should have told me who you were.

You wouldn't have had me then. You would have patted my head and given me candy.

Don't you like candy?

There was a long silence. After a while Soccorro began to cry, at first quietly, disconsolately, then more hysterically, at last deep in her throat, a despairing wail like a Siamese cat. She pummeled him on the chest and stomach until he had to hug her, pinion her arms to protect himself, and it began again.

She left at dawn. Bill lay on his back, staring at the ceiling and pulling on his matted hair. When the sun came up he sighed and fell into an exhausted, restless doze.

Yes, it was just like that. Caitlin remembered the whole agonizing affair, all the months of it, minute by minute, as if it had just ended, and the time since was nothing at all.

□

It was early September. The summer heat had begun to break and the night temperatures were falling into the seventies again. For an hour Caitlin's car had been parked under a tree outside a

condominium in the northeast part of the city. She had followed Porres here, to this unknown woman's apartment. Caitlin wanted to see her, to see some part of Porres's new life. Did
she wear a suit and tie, or have a chignon, or tattooed breasts?

On the last night, after breaking off with Bill, she had sat in
the car, crying and playing country music on the radio until the
station went off the air. Why are some women drawn to older
men? Is it an everyday thing, or is it like a taste for see-through
blouses?

Whatever the reason, it had certainly hurt.

He had never told her anything of himself, but had simply let
her think what she liked. Plenty of people would tell her that
his money came from prostitution and drugs. It was part of his
mystique, part of his power, that he couldn't be bothered to
contradict that. Perhaps it was true: extortion, fraud, murder.
How far was that from the fifties, when he wore black turtle-
neck sweaters and wrote poetry and slept in a bathtub? Not so
far, maybe.

It was really hard to get information on the man, even with
her access to the books and to bank records. She had spent a
good many hours poring over those numbers without being
greatly enlightened. Where had his money come from? It was
difficult, after all that had been said, to accept mere land speculation and an aggressive use of inside information.

Had he kept a diary, or written letters? That seemed so un-
likely.

James Porres emerged out of the passageway to the condominium pool, opened the gate, and locked it again behind him.
To Caitlin's annoyance, he walked casually up to her car and
got in, as matter-of-factly as if he had got out a moment ago to
drop off a package.

Hello, Caitlin, he said, turning to her easily and laying his
hand along the back of the seat. How are you?

Her mouth went suddenly dry.

It's still early, he said. I'd like to drive up Squaw Peak.

He said nothing on the drive, but gazed off to the right, musing on something. He seemed a good deal more dried out than
when she saw him last, at the beginning of the summer. There

was a new assurance, and the small wry smile that once seemed ironic and defeated now was only ironic.

Caitlin parked in a pullout on the mountainside, which gave them a good view of the valley. The air was not so clear and dry as it sometimes was, and the lights below were soft and a little faded. Away to the south, jetliners drifted down, one every two minutes, soundlessly as leaves.

Porres talked quietly about business. Long silences intervened between his sentences. In a small way, he said, he had discovered power. Certainly he was ambitious before. Ambitious to do some quite inconsequential things well. Inconsequential to all but a few. A knowledgeable few. Cognoscenti. Aficionados.

Bill Face had never let himself be cut off. That was the meaning of the changes in him that everyone found so mysterious, so sinister. People find it hard to be anything much. For Bill it was easy.

Porres stroked his chin with the knuckle of his index finger, a new gesture with him. He used to pull his lip or his nose at such times.

When Bill and I started in business, in the bookstore, one of the sacred books of that time was *Walden*. I suppose it's become a college text again, hasn't it? Bill used to buttonhole people about the last chapter. One reads only the first, I think, on economy, and never remembers that he came out of the woods again at the end. Why? Bill wanted to know. He would pretend not to understand, you know, and bleat about it in the silliest way. He used to say that anyone who didn't know the last chapter was a moral midget. Deficient in understanding of good and evil, you see. The last chapter of what? The last chapter. Just the last chapter.

Porres stroked himself under the chin again before going on.

It contributed to his reputation, that way of speaking. That was before your time.

Porres looked directly at Caitlin for the first time since getting into the car.

Bill would never let himself get cut off. I'm getting out of this, he always said. I never heard him talk about getting in.

There was a pause.

He must have got in, of course.

Caitlin wanted to laugh, but the fixity of Porres's gaze prevented her.

Crake was convinced I'd murdered Bill. I was never sure why. Something sordid. I insisted I was innocent. He couldn't prove otherwise, but he kept after me, didn't he? One can't actually prove anything, of course. I should have asked him if he understood the last chapter. Shouldn't I?

This seemed really to require a reply, but Caitlin's tongue was stuck to the roof of her mouth. Porres waited. At last he smiled, faintly and sardonically.

You see I've got through this whole interview, haven't I, without one reference to the pleasant view or the possibilities of our isolation, and the night, and so forth. Just as if we were two old friends.

Yes, Caitlin said.

I think you'd better take me home now. I have a headache.

In the condominium parking lot, Porres did not get out immediately, but stopped with the door open as if he had remembered something. I had a visit from Luther Idge, he said. Quite a young man. I'd advise you to keep your eye on him.

Then he did get out, but paused again with his hand on the door, leaning down to speak through the window.

I don't think I want you to do the books after all, he said. I don't think I should trust you.

And he was gone.

□

They kept him until midnight and then took him to the city jail. He had an idea he could protest this, ought to protest it. But then, he was not charged with any crime, and he supposed the police could hold him overnight if they wished to, on some pretext, for questioning, and since he was not charged, was blameless, perhaps it was beneath his dignity to protest in vain. Perhaps he should have had a lawyer. There had been a lawyer at first, a public defender or someone of that sort. It was in the booking room, or whatever it was called. Scissors. Surely the man's name couldn't have been Scissors? And Lieutenant Crake had taken the man confidentially aside, given him a folded slip of white paper, spoken a few words. What was that about?

There were two other men in the cell in which they left him. The two rapists who had haunted Soccorro's imagination for years had at last found their place. After years of denial, now they would fulfill themselves. In the darkness, like someone trying unobtrusively to open a bag of potato chips, she heard the sound of a zipper—

Hastily, Soccorro turned on the light. A flower of sweat bloomed, with the odor of enfolded skin, enclosed places.

He came home the next morning, haggard and rumpled, during breakfast. With great dignity he sat down at the breakfast table, his hat still on. Her mother got up without a word and left the kitchen, her face white with anger. Soccorro held her ground but drew her robe in a little, hugging herself.

How are you, Daddy?

I'm all right. He took his hat off finally and laid it on the table.

Can I get you something, Daddy?

Coffee.

There was none made. Soccorro spooned some instant into a cup, filled it at the faucet, and heated it in the microwave oven.

What is your mother upset about? he asked blandly, sipping, and went on without expecting an answer. I suppose, he said, she dislikes my being arrested. She's quite right: no one distinguishes true and false arrest. One is distinguished by it. The police know that as well as anyone, of course.

He stood up, leaving his hat and the coffee.

You're not going to work, Daddy? You've been up all night.

Actually, I slept fairly well. And the store must be opened. People will wonder.

Take some breakfast then. A bagel, at least.

He nodded. She got a whole wheat bagel out of the freezer and put it into a plastic bag, which she held out to him. He gazed at her extended hand with curiosity for a time and finally accepted the food.

I've left my bicycle at the store, he asid. I'll take the car to-day. Tell your mother to call me if she needs it.

Your hat.

Soccorro snatched it from the table. It was a tweed cap with a large bill and a button in the center, the sort of cap she had never imagined him wearing.

It's too warm for a hat, he said. Then he was gone.

Soccorro laid the hat on the counter and sat down again at the breakfast table, on a corner of her chair. She tried the coffee, which was bitter and already cold. For several minutes, her thoughts elsewhere, she sat folding up a piece of buttered toast until she had compacted it into a thumb-sized pill which she laid sheepishly in the coffee saucer. Unthinking, she started to lick her greasy fingers, then to wipe them on her robe. Finally she got up for a paper towel.

The dishes should be cleared.

She didn't feel up to it and went out, absently carrying the soiled towel crumpled up in her hand.

□

We ought to go out for a picnic, Porres said on Sunday morning. He had finished the newspaper and was looking through the sliding screen out into the back yard, a cup of coffee in his hand. Isela flicked her eyes over the back of her husband's head and said nothing. She buttered another piece of toast. First a bicycle, now a picnic. She supposed it had something to do with spring, or middle-age. Isela had been spared that crisis so far, having got to middle-age directly from adolescence. Perhaps in another few years she would find out, with menopause, what the panic was.

It will be too hot for a picnic soon, Porres observed.

What did you have in mind, then?

Porres shrugged. Just to go over to the park, I suppose.

Such a scruffy place. Isela brushed crumbs of toast from her fingers.

Encanto Park, then. Remember we used to take Soccorro when she was little. We haven't been there for years.

Soccorro padded in half dressed and went to the refrigerator for a glass of milk.

Your father wants to have a picnic, dear.

Fun. She turned, wiping the milk from her upper lip with the back of her hand. Let's go up Peralta Canyon. I know a nice place there.

Such a drive, Isela murmured.

No farther than Encanto Park, Porres said, siding against her.

Isela conceded and got up to pack a lunch. Soccorro ambled off to get dressed, leaving the refrigerator door open. Smiling, Porres turned back to his contemplation of the back yard.

I ought to cut the grass, he said after a time. Isela was opening a package of sandwich meat.

You didn't call Mr. Phillips yet, did you.

No.

I don't suppose you could use some legal advice.

No.

Porres abruptly put down his cup. I'm going to change my clothes, he said. And shave.

At ten o'clock they were on the road—the freeway, and then the deep fringe of trailer parks and billboards which thinned out after twenty miles more until at last they were out on the desert, beginning to climb up one of the long fingers of the valley into the dry mountains. Before long Soccorro directed them to turn off. Another half hour's driving over a dirt road scored by runoff, with the windows rolled up against the dust, brought them to a shadeless, barren spot at the foot of purple dacite cliffs, among palo verde and pale green cholla and one yucca.

Do you come here much? he wanted to know.

Soccorro shrugged. Some.

Popular with kids, I suppose. Porres looked over the cars standing in the parking lot. Jeeps and small trucks. A Bug with a naked engine and an exhaust sticking up like a skunk's tail. He looked up the canyon where they had all gone. A few hundred feet ahead was the picnic area, deserted.

He looked back, down the road. Laid out below their feet to the west was a corner of the valley, seeming only roughly settled at this distance, with only roads and low buildings and a few palms visible. The canyon through which they had come lay hidden in a fold of the mountains that stood in rising imbrications to the horizon. Dragon's scales.

Isela had already unpacked the lunch. Eggs, sandwiches, lemonade. No salt. No napkins. No cups.

Let us admire the work of God.

Must we?

What else is admirable?

It's a hundred and ten degrees.

It's ninety-five.

It feels like a hundred and ten.

Rather, with polite silence, Porres ate an egg and confined himself to a brief gesture with his sandwich. The egg was dry and stuck in his throat.

I want to go for a walk, Soccorro said when lunch was over.

Porres got to his feet. Are you coming, Isela?

No.

Come on, Mom.

Take a shirt, girl. You'll burn.

Soccorro accepted the shirt but did not put it on. Isela began to repack the picnic things as she watched her daughter scramble away up the trail. The child would never burn—she had too much free time to lie naked on the grass in the back yard. Skin like bacon already. Cancer. Thirty pounds of skin cancer. And running shoes without socks to go hiking in.

You'll burn, Daddy.

Soccorro held out the shirt, which Porres slipped on over his own thin white one. His pale forearms, exposed by short sleeves, were already beginning to redden beneath the sparse black hair.

You should have brought a hat.

He shrugged. We won't be long.

A fourth of a mile up the canyon was a stopping place, a flat rock under the striated shade of a palo verde. In a small clearing on the other side of the trail were the remains of a campfire and a few crushed beer cans. Porres sat down. His leather-soled shoes had been slipping in the gravel and he had scraped the knee of his trousers.

Honestly, Daddy. When was the last time you were out in the desert?

Porres looked up, smiling. I don't know as I ever was, he said.

What?

I sell books, he said, and shrugged. What reason would I have to come here? Where I was a boy the countryside was all ploughed and fenced. I'd have been shot. And by the time I moved here I was grown up.

There was a long silence. Porres admired the dry desert landscape. In the shelter of the canyons it was surprisingly lush.

Do they really suspect you, then?

Of what?

Soccorro gaped at her father, incredulous.

Of murder, she said at last.

Oh.

Porres stood up. Yes, I suppose they do.

Why did you— were you supposed to have done it?

I don't know.

Was it jealousy? Because Mother was sleeping with him?

Porres flushed and looked at his hands. I suppose, he said, that does count for something with the authorities. Actually, they seem to think it was more to do with money. Jealousy, perhaps— no, envy. Envy of his success. Do people really think me a failure?

Soccorro made no reply.

Ah. Well, I don't yet see what I gain by Bill's death. A provision in his will? It seems unlike him to have made a will. Perhaps I'll be found to have stolen some great sum, which he was on the point of discovering.

Did you? This light way of speaking irritated Soccorro.

I don't think so. Perhaps I was a silent partner in Bill's speculations. What do you think? The actual grey eminence, even, protected from public scrutiny behind the appearance of a fool?

Daddy.

Porres shrugged. Bill threatened to discard me, you know. Or no: was it that he stupidly tried to go out on his own, like Phaidon in the Sun's chariot, and jeopardized everything? Well,

I suppose the police are no more ignorant of people's real motivations than the rest of us. One can invent a plausible explanation for anything.

I must say, Porres went on after a time, I don't think the police understand my business arrangements with Bill. If Bill's speculations had come down around his ears, you know I would have lost the shop.

Porres looked at his hands. I was hardly in danger. Bill was quite good, really. Quite good.

But Daddy, these accusations are false.

Porres frowned. Oh no, he said, taking her arm. Insofar as they fit the facts there is quite a bit in them.

Daddy!

Shall we go up a little farther?

They walked arm in arm, slowly, Porres picking his way more carefully than before.

The authorities' ideas don't yet fit the facts very well, of course. But it wouldn't do for me to turn my eyes away from my shortcomings, since no one else will overlook them.

But you're innocent.

Yes, in the legal sense, I suppose I am. Morally also, perhaps. But what is that? You are innocent, eh? An innocent child? Suppose I impute to you some horrible crime. How would you defend yourself? Of what use is your innocence? Someone, a rejected lover perhaps—that boy you were seeing last year—

Oh!

—makes false accusations against you. You point out the motive behind his accusations, suggest his interest in misrepresenting the facts, cast doubts on his character, and so forth. And if you are not believed? Suppose your accuser has no such motives. If he is only a man on the bus who habitually thinks the worst of everyone, who imagines you to be a slut guilty of unimaginable crimes because you are young and pretty—

Soccorro stopped, feeling faint. She should have brought a hat for herself. Her father turned, but looked past her, unaware of her distress, down into the canyon.

Have you been here very many times, Soccorro?

A few times. With friends.

Men friends?

Well, for parties, you know.

Mmm.

After a moment they went on up the trail and Porres fell again to musing.

In times past, he said, you might have taken such accusations seriously. You would have lived in fear lest you give anyone reason to doubt your virtue, which after all is a fragile thing. The loss of it would mean complete ruin. You dressed in vast loose clothes, were cool and haughty, and the more you hid the more you were thought to be hiding. There is no defense.

Time passed.

In the heat of the day the desert was so quiet that it had begun to disturb him. He scuffed his feet.

You won't do anything, then?

Why encourage them?

Why let them?

Soccorro, who would want to live in such a world?

You won't defend yourself?

No. Your mother will be upset with me, I imagine. But you know, all her best crockery has been smashed already.

The trail had been climbing steadily up the western side of the canyon and now they stood high enough to see its length, from the Fremont Saddle which closed the upper end a mile above, to the parking lot a mile and a half below. Isela had apparently gone to sit in the car. On the other side of the canyon a couple appeared over the ridge and began to pick their way down the steeper eastern trail toward a shallow cave in the canyon wall. Farther up near the saddle, where rock buttresses stood like the deep encrusted drips of wax on a candlestick, the western wall was already in shadow, and in fifteen minutes the trail deeper in the canyon would also be dark. The opposite wall, its rim crenelated with saguaro and yucca spikes against the hot blue sky, now took the full force of the sun. The two climbers had disappeared into the shadow of the cave. Some way below, the rock fell away in a smooth steep face covered with a brilliant verdigris lichen. Over this a man with a rope was making his way, a spot of brilliant orange. Still farther down, the canyon opened out into the upper valley, still green, seeming almost forested. By summer it would all be slag and cinders, he supposed, the waste of some vast forge lifted into a sky so deep, so transparent that it promised nothing.

Very nice, he said again.

A slight breeze stirred Soccorro's hair.

Daddy—

No, no, safer to keep counsel, to be quiet.

Yes?

I'm going back.

Porres nodded. I'll come along in a bit.

He watched her go. She ran with long strides, twice stumbled, once fell. Then she was gone from sight. After a moment he followed, walking slowly, his eyes on the trail.

An hour later, when he returned to the parking lot he found it empty. Two dust-covered cars remained, neither one his. In the utter silence the little breeze arose again, almost too light a breeze to feel, a little vagary with a distant odor of ozone.

He was given a ride into town by a man in an empty truck, who observed his passenger's city shoes and sunburned face without comment.

Breakdown?

Yes.

Take you as far as a phone. Send out a wrecker.

That would be fine. Thank you.

In town he thought of calling home, but hung up after three rings. It was evening by the time he trudged up the curving street to his darkened house. A gray government car sat in the driveway, from which Lieutenant Crake emerged.

Where are my wife and daughter? asked Porres sharply.

I have no idea. Crake's voice was quiet. He seemed surprised.

How long have you been here?

Just an hour.

Is this an official visit?

Crake laughed, a dry snuffling noise, but made no reply.

Inside, Porres filled two glasses with cold water from the refrigerator and carried them into the living room where Crake had installed himself.

I would prefer to sit in the dark, I think, Crake said. It's cooler.

Porres nodded. The room was stuffy from having been shut up all day. He was having trouble breathing.

Please sit down, James. You're exhausted. It's my fault; I should have sent a man out to get you.

Ah?

Certainly, it would be foolish of me not to keep an eye out, not to keep myself informed. But I don't like to interfere. Would you like to shower?

No.

You ought. It gives me an unnecessary advantage. As you wish. Do I understand that your wife has left you?

I don't remember saying so.

No, perhaps not.

Porres sat down stiffly on the edge of the sofa, while Crake reclined at ease in the chair opposite, his feet up on the ottoman. Now, said Crake, sipping from his glass, what I have in mind is this. It seems that your William Face was a considerable man. More considerable, I think, than is generally known. These things have a way of coming out, of course—afterwards. Haven't they?

Crake made an inviting pause, but Porres, who a moment before had felt strangled, suddenly quit struggling and collapsed. Exhaustion, he observed of himself with curiosity. He was a sedentary man, easily exhausted. Why had he not begun to prepare himself earlier?

Yes, he managed. A way of coming out.

You understand, Crake went on, I would prefer not to wait so long.

So Isela had left him. Where was Soccorro? He felt paralyzed, drained of will, as by a snake's eye. Crake seemed to be waiting for a reply.

Yes.

Good. Crake drank again and put the glass down on the table at his elbow. He had provided himself with a coaster somehow. Porres didn't know where the coasters were kept. That had always been Isela's business. She had never trusted him with the house, trusted him to keep up appearances.

Crake was going over Bill's business arrangements. There had always been some uncertainty as to how Bill came by his money, some faint Faustian odor. It was his love of secrecy, intrigue. He was the sort of man who would hide the light switch in the bathroom. Yet he had begun as a poet, uncomplicated, a pleasure-lover. Faust was a man of principle.

It was hard to know what to make of Bill Face. He seemed not to have scrupled over his acquaintances. If Uncle Remus, sent up a few years ago for dealing in stolen goods, or Mr. Toad, convicted of procurement, or Jack Horner, under suspicion of bribery and tax fraud, were all his friends, did that mean that he was the center of a ring of thieves and whoremasters, and that power had been unfairly brought to bear for his benefit? Apparently it did. He had taken such trouble to obscure the origins of the land, the money, the expensive clothes and the rest, without taking any trouble at all to allay suspicion, as if he had wanted to appear to the world a great Moriarty and not a broken-down bohemian, the owner of a bookshop.

Crake began chewing an ice cube. Porres remained silent.

It seemed there were a great many people with sufficient motive and opportunity to have murdered Bill Face. Perhaps this is true of anyone. It is only necessary for a man to die in the middle of the night, in ordinary circumstances, unobserved. The sources of hatred, envy, and greed are ubiquitous. Who is able to prove his innocence in the middle of the night? It is only because there are not enough murders to go around that more people are not accused.

There is a shortage of accusers, too, Porres said, rousing himself.

Crake smiled. Indeed. Everyday crime is such a dull affair. The easiest thing is to keep a crowd of small-time hoods, a few frozen dinners, you know, for the times when you can't be bothered to cook. Eh? Efficient use of the public funds.

But Porres had sunk back into apathy. Crake began to think he had made a mistake. He had hoped to break his man, but Porres was too limp to break. Unless he were one of those who goes to sleep under pressure. That would make things difficult.

The routine accusations, of course, would hardly give satisfaction in such a case as this one, even if they were true. It was necessary to go shopping, as it were, for something fresh. Rufus Woyke, perhaps. The front man, every bit as furtive and sullen as befits a man whose purpose is to protect secrets. A means for Face to launder assets. A henchman. And Bill could never have let him go, with all his dangerous knowledge. He would have had to be put away. Woyke would protect himself, of course . . .

Certainly a prosaic hypothesis, rather like business as usual. There were other possibilities: Isela Porres, Bill's long-time paramour. An antique word, paramour, but appropriate. One never has to look far for a lover's motive. In bed, hoping to make it seem a heart attack, but she misjudged, struck too hard. So it would be better if the corpse were moved to another venue. Carry it down to the store, arrange appearances, lock up and walk home. Had no one seen her? Perhaps.

Caitlin Vachon. She fucks, of course. They all do. Bill never passed up a chance to buy for stock, did he? He could always take her off the shelf if he wanted a bank spy. And if she refused?

Soccorro Porres.

Crake's opponent got slowly to his feet. He spoke with an effort, as if he were not used to it.

I don't think I will be of any use to you this evening, he said. Another time, perhaps.

Lieutenant Crake cracked the last bit of ice with his teeth and rose to go. Yes, he said. Another time. It has been a pleasant chat. Not very informative, but pleasant. Get some rest, James. You needn't show me out. I can find my own way.

Yes, I imagine you can.

Crake smiled in acknowledgment.

Say nothing, Porres thought when Crake had gone. Keep quiet. That's the way.

□

Caitlin Vachon, if she were to go any further, had to find out more. Reconstruct more of what Crake had known, what he had intended. She sought out the patrolman Francis Tuchman. He was not particularly eager to talk. The Face business was something he should never have been involved in. It had embarrassed the department and cost him a promotion. And his involvement was only by happenstance, he insisted. Only happenstance.

Tuchman lived near the river, in what Caitlin thought of as a working-class neighborhood. The houses were thirty years old, going back to the first post-war development boom, and were beginning to show the cardboard nature of slap-up desert housing. Caitlin was struck again by the speed with which things age in the desert. The lawns were patchy and tired, the bushes struggling. The houses were too old for central air conditioning. They had not been built for it, and most had a dripping, rusty box poked into a bedroom window instead, propped up with a board. One room—the bedroom—refrigerated, and the rest of the house in the nineties with the musty dampness of swamp cooling. At least they could have the windows open. Every summer Caitlin had a continuous sinus headache from air conditioning. She longed to have the windows open, to work with hot air and street sounds and grit, to watch the papers blow off her desk. But her desk was nowhere near a window, which could not be opened in any case.

The Tuchmans' rooms were too small, too full. Whenever she moved she bumped into something: a chair with projecting arms, plaques on the wall, scattered toys, the corner of a rug turned up. Several children were screaming at the back of the house. Four old people sat in a row on the living room couch, three women and a man. Tuchman's wife, a scrawny barefoot woman

74

smoking a cigarette, emerged from another room and, appraising Caitlin harshly, went away to pour cold tea.

Caitlin felt like a social worker. Tuchman took her off toward the back, past the bathroom and through a bedroom into the yard where the children were playing with a plastic bat and ball. Two sides of the narrow yard were protected by immense oleander hedges and the back, on the alley, was blocked by a chain link fence with a padlocked gate. A spindly grapefruit tree about six feet high, bearing thirty or so green fruit, grew at the edge of the cement patio. A small metal table and chairs stood nearby, in the shade of the oleanders. Tuchman gestured to her to sit. His wife came out with three glasses of sun tea.

Caitlin could not believe the Tuchmans were actually poor. How much did a patrolman make? Twenty thousand? It was the way they lived. There were too many children, too many old people. Caitlin wasn't used to disorder, was she? She was inclined to confuse it with squalor. Her distaste for all this—the overgrown lawn, the children, the scarred linoleum and the rubble—had been rather transparent, hadn't it? Embarrassed, she found it difficult to begin.

Tuchman, however, was quite unconcerned. He had no intention of talking to her, or to anyone, about the Face business. Why should he? And flapping his lip now would be a good way of making sure he was passed over a second time, wouldn't it?

Crake's superiors didn't object to your involvement? You're a patrolman, after all. You shouldn't have been asked, should you?

Why should they object, if the job gets done? There had never been complaints about him. The job got done, no one complained. Why should they?

Caitlin, a little non-plussed, scrutinized the young patrolman's face for signs of irony. In vain. His wife seemed to be hiding a little bitter smile, though, behind her glass of tea.

This case was different, surely? Crake had a personal interest in this case, didn't he?

I suppose so. Tuchman sipped from his own glass of tea.

He was convinced of Porres's guilt from the start. Why?

Tuchman shrugged. After a moment he said: I don't know.

He was. She insisted: he was. I was there when he first came into the store. So were you. It was like my neighbor's dog—instinctive. What have I ever done to that dog? Nothing. Why? A smell; some guilty stain which Crake saw with the third eye, glowing like a scorpion at night?

Tuchman shrugged again. I wasn't going to say anything about this, was I? I shouldn't have invited you in, only I know you. What's your interest in this now, Miss Vachon?

A hard plastic ball the size of a grapefruit bounced onto the table between them and hit Mrs. Tuchman on the cheek. She glared.

Come on, Frank, she said. You're trying to pretend it's all over. They know you, Frank. It's on your record. They might have done something for you, but they didn't. Why is that?

Tuchman winced. Self-consciously he began to wipe dirt from the table top with his index finger.

Lieutenant Crake kept pretty well to himself, he said after a time. Why should he talk to me? Who knows what he said to the Captain?

Things get around though, he admitted.

What did Crake know at the end? How far had he come?

Tuchman did not reply.

But he must have told you what to expect?

I don't think he knew himself.

Mrs. Tuchman snorted. He expected to find the gun, Frank. If he had found Porres with the gun he could have shot him dead. Self-defense.

What gun, Tuchman muttered.

The gun Bill went up on the ladder to get, said Caitlin.

No gun, Tuchman replied stubbornly.

What?

No one has ever produced the gun, ma'am. It was nothing but marks in the dust. The Lieutenant said there had been a gun. No one saw a gun.

Caitlin cleared her throat uncertainly. But he fell, she began. The blood on the desk—

Cat blood.

What? He told James—

The Lieutenant wanted to put a little pressure on Mr. Porres, I think. He knew it was a murder. He was always convinced of that, wasn't he? The evidence was a little thin. You have to start somewhere.

The evidence was a little thin.

Why do you suppose it was hushed up? If he had broken Porres do you suppose any questions would have been asked? There would have been plenty of evidence then.

Sitting in her car after the interview, she had looked back toward the house to see Tuchman standing at the living room window, talking to someone unseen. Again and again he ran his fingers through his hair, and at last he turned away from the window.

Why did the case seem so complicated? What had there been about Bill Face that his death should cause so much confusion?

So Crake had manufactured evidence.

Well, no. That wasn't so. The Lieutenant had simply not told her all the facts. And why should he?

How fatuous of her to think she would be able to find out. As a child she had simply waited to be told. She had gone to church and waited, gloved hands folded in her lap. But no one told her anything, and she had come to feel there was nothing to learn.

As if anyone could be bothered.

Her faith must have been very shallow, mustn't it, to be shaken by a little puzzle like this? Who killed Bill Face? No one knows. Was it really such an offense, not to have been told? An offense of God against Man?

But it was true. There were things she hadn't been told.

How fatuous to have thought otherwise.

No gun. Cat's blood. Why so much trouble to create the appearance of an accident, and yet bungle it?

Perhaps it had been an accident after all? Early that morning, about one o'clock, Bill had stopped by the bookstore for some pocket money, as he was in the habit of doing. The wino saw them go in. Bill was a little drunk, perhaps. The ladder was not in good repair. Soccorro panicked and ran. She couldn't afford to be involved. Why had he wanted the gun, though? Hadn't they argued? Hadn't she pushed over the ladder when she saw that he had a gun? No, she couldn't have it known. She took the gun and fled. She took the car and the gun and ran to Woyke for help, the only person she could trust. And he hid the gun for her, picked up her car at Bill's house, went back to lock up. Would he have gone inside? Probably not. There was too great a danger of leaving traces. There were the two sets of tire tracks, of course. That couldn't be helped. The police would conclude that Bill had come back later, by himself, and Soccorro would be in the clear. In the dark, Woyke might have been mistaken for Bill Face that second time, coming back to clean up. If anyone had noticed— But no one had.

And then Crake, against the grain, decided to investigate. Why? He was old; his instincts had betrayed him. It was always done by instinct and probability, after all. They had had an argument. A torn scrap of her blouse was found in his hand. Under her nails there was skin from his face, and in her purse a little gun. She said the Devil did it. Who wants to believe that?

So Crake, meddling, had threatened to discover the truth. Even then, she would have been safe if only Crake hadn't suspected her father. How could she tell her father?

Caitlin tried to imagine the sequence of panic, despair, and moral paralysis that had brought Soccorro to the end. And who was the poor man with the Volkswagen? Some little fellow leading a pitiful double life, a dreary bourgeois existence which he tried to palliate with desperate encounters in sleazy bars? A closet pedophile, an aging cowboy. Crake had known, of course, from the auto registration. He had gone out to Cave Creek or Glendale or wherever, she felt sure, and ruined the man. For nothing. What did he know? He had picked her up in a bar once, balled her in the parking lot. Nothing kinky. Just fast and cold. He'd been a little depressed for a couple of days afterward. Then he met her again, by chance. Well of course, if you go the rounds of the same bars every week you're bound to see the same people.

He'd been standing alone, drinking and watching the band. She surprised him from behind, wanted to go to the dog track for some reason. He hadn't objected. She seemed a little pale.

Maybe she was speeding a bit. He supposed she had taken something. They often do that, to get their nerve up.

He shrugged. Sometimes it's better that way, sometimes worse.

He'd been looking for a good time, actually. She went back for her purse. After about three races he began to wonder. Called a taxi finally. An arm and a leg, yes. He never did find out what happened until now. He'd been thinking of reporting it, of course, the stolen car. Only he would have to admit he'd been to the track . . .

He didn't remember her having a purse, no.

But on Monday morning, under the fluorescent lights of Caitlin's office, with her white porcelain mug full of sharp pencils and a stack of economic forecasts to abstract for a ten o'clock meeting, things did not seem so neat as they had the day before.

Crake had been obsessed with the gun. Why, if there was no gun? Why had someone wanted to invent a gun?

Suppose there had been a gun. Woyke's, perhaps, with Soccorro's fingerprints on it, lying on the floor after she fled. And Woyke had made it appear, if the gun should ever turn up, that it was Bill's and not his. So that the evidence would not be overlooked, he tinkered with the fallen books.

Cat's blood.

Bizarre subtlety on the one hand, stupidity on the other. As if the whole scene had been manufactured from scratch for the sole purpose of calling attention to itself without giving anything away.

A raspberry. Pthlbthbthlblb in her face.

Caitlin pulled the stack of economic reports toward her. The top one, in its antiseptic plastic binder, slipped off onto the floor.

Amateur detectives, she thought, bending over to get the report, might get shot. Straightening, she cracked her head on the underside of the desk.

What did she really know about Bill Face? Perhaps he had, after all, been the grey eminence of a subtle web of power. He had had power, certainly. Might those others not use it now to protect themselves? She hoped not. She wanted not to believe in the existence of secrets, in things hidden, in the falseness of appearances. She wanted to go on thinking that evil was done mostly by sincere wrongheaded men and bumblers with good intentions. She wanted to think that bestsellers could never be any good and that people who made themselves sick over interest rates or threats of nuclear war had gotten their priorities upside down. She wanted to believe it was in bad taste to try to make people cry in movie theatres. She wanted to believe that you could love more than one person at a time, and that doctors mostly don't know what they are doing, and that you could think it was all worth it without having to believe in God.

Somehow that didn't seem so unreasonable. Modest, even.

She got out one of the familiar yellow pads from the desk, took up one of the reports and, still rubbing the top of her head, began to make her notes for the meeting.

At lunch, after the meeting, she looked at the notes again, bent over them at a tiny table in the far corner of a sub shop. The tiny square table was hardly large enough for a beer and the sandwich which dripped oil into the paper boat in which it had been served. An overhead fan lifted the sheets of yellow legal paper now entirely covered with her minuscule scribbling. She used the sweating beer glass to hold the papers down.

Everyone was willing to try a hand at forecasting the economy, it seemed. Their conclusions were wildly different, even contradictory. The more she learned about the several forecasters the more apparent it was to her that the whole process was mainly one of finding plausible reasons for what was at bottom a well-developed sense of poetic justice. And each economist distributed his praise and blame according to his own agon, his preferences in catastrophe. Some of these systems sniveled and died, some blew up, some went around and around.

By the time Caitlin had finished eating, her papers were soaked with oil. She wadded them up along with the sandwich wrapping paper and threw everything away. The meeting had been a success.

She'd eaten too fast. She always did when she had a submarine sandwich for lunch. The sub shop was too crowded to let her relax.

A walk would settle her stomach, she thought, and she headed over a block in order to pass by Woyke's old shop on the way back to the office. It was empty, as usual. Luther Idge was going to go belly up with it, but there was nothing remarkable about that. There never had been. Nobody could make a living with that shop.

She decided to speak to Luther. Soon. After work.

□

It was, however, nearly two weeks before Caitlin was able to talk to Luther. On the first try, there was no one in the shop. The sound of a radio came from a vacant back room. The next evening she caught an ancient indolent clerk emerging from the back room with a cup of coffee.

I'd like to see Mr. Idge.

Gone home, the clerk mumbled, trying to duck back into the storeroom.

Will he be in tomorrow?

Far as I know.

But he wasn't. Every evening for a week she stopped in with no luck. She became adept at winkling the clerk out of his hiding places.

What time does he go home?

Depends.

Has he been in today?

No ma'am.

Has he been in all week?

No ma'am.

When do you expect him?

Can't say.

Could you let me have his home address?

Is it business?

Yes, it is.

Mr. Idge's give me orders not to send anyone on business, ma'am.

And the next week the shop was closed.

Her banking sources produced a telephone number and address, but when she called to make an appointment she got only an answering machine and was reluctant to leave a message for fear of alarming him. At last she took an afternoon and drove around to his house.

Luther Idge was living considerably above his means, it was clear. It was also clear that he had not been home in some time. There was a notice on the door from the development office warning him about the condition of his lawn, and when she rang the bell a dog began to hurl itself against the other side of the door, barking hysterically. She peeked into the mailbox, and thought for a moment about going around to the back, but as it was the sort of development likely to have its own security, and she had been too curious already, it seemed safer to give up. And when she tried the telephone number again, it had been disconnected.

At last, by keeping careful watch, she caught him one night loading some office machines into a station wagon at the back of the shop.

Certainly. What harm could there be in a little chat? But not here. Get in. I've got a place around the corner.

Luther's place was a shack. The front of the building was entirely hidden by a ten-foot hedge of prickly pears. A dead palm tree stood next door, in a vacant lot dotted with mesquite and desert broom. The palm looked as if it were about to fall on the house. Luther parked alongside the building and backed up to the fence. Through a gate he unloaded the office equipment into the back yard and from there carried it inside.

Get you a beer? he asked, bringing a six-pack from the car.

Sure.

There was nowhere to sit. The three rooms were filled with old bicycles, used stereo equipment and ancient televisions, adding machines, and hundreds of other objects jumbled like a pawnshop after an earthquake.

Do you live here?

Hell no, he called out from the kitchen. That wouldn't be smart, would it? he added, emerging with two slightly warm cans of beer. He opened his own, dropped the tab on the floor, and drank half of it. Hey look, he said. You got to start some-

where. Even L. Bill Face had to start dealing from some part of
the deck. What was it you wanted?

Caitlin popped her beer and let the foam slide onto the floor.
I think you forgot to feed your dog, she said.

Luther blinked, and then grinned with comprehension. Not
my dog, he said.

Ah. I'm sorry to see you couldn't keep the bookshop going.
Enh.

I think you went to Mr. Porres for some help? And he threw
you out. What was that about?

Porres. That righteous ass. Are you from him?

No. I'm on my own.

You and he being so close, I thought for a minute he might
of reconsidered. Stupid of me. No consideration, none at all.

Caitlin demurred. We're not particularly close, as a matter of
fact.

Do tell.

I have an idea James Porres is responsible for Bill's death.
Mixed up in it somehow. He told me you had been in to see
him. What was it you asked him for?

Luther stared at the rotting ceiling. In the darkening room
the bicycles and the heaps of equipment became a shadowed
mass, and Caitlin felt like a child in a secret clubhouse.

Rufus Woyke had this arrangement with Bill Face, Luther
said at last. I suggested to Porres that it might be worth his
while to continue it.

What arrangement?

Porres said he didn't know anything about that and slammed
the door in my face. I don't suppose he did know, the sanctimonious bastard.

What was the arrangement?

Luther gazed at Caitlin out of the side of his eye. He drank
off the rest of his beer and threw the can into a corner.

I don't know, he admitted. I was hoping to feel it out of Porres. Look here. Woyke's shop was always in the red. Face
made that good every month. Woyke had other little things
from him, too. I don't know—hot tips, women? You know.
Face would stop by every couple of weeks and sit in the back

with his feet up like a damn cowboy, and Woyke'd be there with his hands in his lap, stiff upright in that black suit he always wore. I don't suppose it was what it looked like. A couple of sharp operators, those two.

You never heard anything of what they said to each other?

Luther stood up and ambled toward the window. He lifted one of the sheets of newsprint covering the glass and gazed for a time across the vacant lot and into the street. Then he let the paper fall.

Payment for past services, maybe, he said. For old times sake, you know. Getting dark, isn't it? You want to move outside? The electricity's off in here.

He pushed open the screen and went out without waiting for an answer. Caitlin put her warm beer down on a television and followed. They sat on an old cable reel, leaned back against the wall of the house and looked over the city toward the desert to the south. A band of bright stars stood low in the sky in that direction, stars which were obscured overhead by the streetlights. Off to the right lay the dark bulk of South Mountain with its forest of red-lit television towers. At the foot of the mountain a new resort had put up a tall pier festooned with yellow lights. Here and there across the valley floor squares of intense white marked baseball diamonds and tennis courts, like sheets of newspaper blown into an empty lot. Overhead, jetliners on the Sky Harbor flight path rumbled past every two minutes.

Let's call it blackmail, Caitlin said. For convenience. Though I don't think Bill would have let himself be put at any serious disadvantage.

Serious enough to get himself killed.

It might have been an accident.

You don't say.

What was it Woyke and Face talked about at those times? Or don't you know?

No.

Any ideas?

Nn.

For a time Luther said nothing more. Then he got up to

fetch a second beer. I have an idea, he said when he had settled himself beside her again, that Woyke burned something there at the end. Business records, I suppose. Something from the old days, maybe? An address list. Photographs. I don't know.

Bill had that reputation, didn't he?

Hey listen, you got to start somewhere. Else how'd he get his money? You don't get it out of a bookstore. Bookstores eat money. You can't tell me, fifteen twenty years ago, that some damn beatnik could make enough on poetry readings and philosophy to buy half of downtown, even if it was falling down, which it was.

There are a lot of ways to get money.

Why didn't he ever say so, then? If he was so straight why would he want people saying all that about him?

It must have been hard to blackmail Bill if he paid so little attention to his reputation, don't you think?

Well, I don't suppose it was himself he was protecting so much. I guess it was Porres.

Oh?

You can't blackmail that sonofabitch. He just gets his back up. Innocent as a newborn lamb, he says. Innocent as the Pope, I think. You could hurt him, maybe, if you had the right stuff. But there's no money in it.

Caitlin mused over this for a while before deciding to go on with what did not seem a very useful interview. When she spoke again it was to take a new line, which she hoped would be more plausible and less lurid than blackmail.

Did Woyke want to stop the investigation?

Sure.

Why?

Come on. To save the women and children, what do you think? Because Crake was going to hang the murder on him, that's why.

But Crake was dead against Jim Porres, wasn't he? What evidence was there?

How can you tell? Whatever Woyke was getting money for, there wasn't going to be any more of it. He was being set up. As soon as Crake brought the gun home to him, and all that messing around with the body, it would be pretty clear, wouldn't it?

What messing about? You can't move a corpse without its being known.

How about the trick with the blood?

Cat's blood.

Luther turned to her. Do tell, he said after a time. But there's still the girl.

Soccorro?

That's the one. Convenient to have her kept so quiet, wasn't it.

Caitlin made a deprecating noise. She was beginning to be uncomfortable.

Oh, Luther said, a little smugly, I guess he leaned on her anyway. I guess Crake leaned on her too. Between the two of them they talked her into it, I guess.

Caitlin squirmed. She had had her own run-ins with Crake, but this was a sordid idea. It was far too easy for people like Luther Idge to imagine this comic-book violence against the soft bodies of women. It was too much like little boys cutting up worms and frogs. Still, Crake had been callous in his pursuit of information. No more so than a credit officer, perhaps? And as a tactic it would probably have been a good way to corner Soccorro. Caitlin recalled her own teens. She had been a raw egg then.

So you ran to him for help, Crake observed, a little edge to his voice. And what was the price?

She said nothing. He laughed.

Fucked you good, didn't he?

She closed her eyes to keep control a little longer.

Kinky bitch.

But he would have played the same line against Woyke, too.

Damn right, Luther said. Accused him of rape.

Just a little joke between the boys, I suppose?

That's right. But Woyke took it seriously, anyhow. He was white. It was only a matter of time before Crake did for him.

Caitlin gazed off into the night sky.

Well, Luther added uneasily. He was in it pretty deep after all.

Was he.

She closed her eyes, suddenly out of patience. She wanted to break the case in a physical, literal way—over her knee, rip it open like the gut of an animal cornered at last. She supposed Crake had felt that way, too. It must be a common thing for detectives, a feeling they would have to learn to deal with eventually.

Did Crake know about Soccorro from the first?

Had to know, Luther replied. He finished his second beer.

Had to, of course. A few routine inquiries in the bars would turn her up.

□

Soccorro shifted uneasily on her chair. The plastic upholstery made her legs sweat. She had begun by lighting a cigarette to appear calm, but it had made her sick. The long stub lay now in a clean ashtray, the only object on the polished table top. She shifted her hands on the table, leaving irregular splotches of perspiration.

Lieutenant Crake observed the questioning from the darkness, leaning against a large walnut desk, idly pressing the buttons on a telephone. In the circle of lamplight a lean young man in a three-piece suit was taking her statement.

She had been with Bill. They never went out, but this once she had persuaded him to take her to a jazz club. They left about midnight, just before the last set. He said he wanted to stop for cash. She waited a long time in the car. Perhaps ten minutes.

You went in then.

He was lying on the floor by the stock ladder.

You ran. Where?

Home.

Your car was at Bill's. How did you get home?

I walked.

It's three miles. And you left your car?

I went up later to get it.

You didn't think of calling a doctor?

No.

Did you think he was dead, then?

Yes.

What was he doing on the stock ladder? Were there books pulled down from the shelf?

Yes. Three or four. Several books. A dozen, maybe.

A dozen books on the floor. As if he had fallen and pulled them down.

Yes.

And he hadn't been looking into the desk? Were there papers out, or a ledger, or a cash box?

No.

What had he gone in for, then?

Soccorro's mouth was dry. She reached for the broken cigarette in the ashtray and began to shred it. The inquisitor ceased writing and laid down his pencil.

There were papers on the floor in the morning, he said. The typescript of one of your father's catalogs, I believe.

Crake confirmed this with a grunt.

Soccorro finished shredding the cigarette and folded her hands. After a long wait the inquisitor picked up his pencil again.

There were two sets of tire tracks in the parking lot behind the store, both made by Bill's car. If we are to accept your statement, the second set must have been made after his death.

She had taken the car, yes. To go after her own.

Who brought it back? Who locked up the store? Do you have a key?

Yes.

I see. You locked the store to hide the fact that you had been there, to make it appear as if Bill had locked the door himself after going in, as he would have done if he were alone.

Yes.

Why? If he had only fallen down, what could you be accused of?

Well, he wad dead, you see. Wasn't he.

I don't know. Was he?

Soccorro tried to remove a few shreds of tobacco which were

sticking to her damp fingers. After a long silence the inspector began again.

And again. That much was certain, Caitlin thought. Crake had had the essential facts in his hand from the beginning. And yet it was impossible to say for certain what happened.

But wasn't that always the case? One never knew the whole of anything. There was always a backside, like a conjurer's other hand—always something else going on. There was always another explanation, even for something so simple as reaching for the salt.

Well, perhaps never was a bit strong. Wasn't it obvious that people were mostly in agreement about things? About whether there was salt on the table, and so forth?

Caitlin remembered a graduate seminar on public policy she had audited in her senior year, while she was still thinking she might go on for another degree. She had been told to investigate the demographics of voter turnout in the last decade. So many people voted in Colorado, so many in California. What did that mean? Nothing, it seemed. Were there more people voting now than ten years ago? Uncertain. More old people? How many Hispanics? Impossible to say. How many Hispanics are there, anyway? On some questions she had found estimates as divergent as forty percent. She began to wonder what people in government were thinking of when they announced plans for this or that.

There had been another paper in that same class, on government regulation of the pharmaceutical industry, read by a thin freckle-faced man whose liberal politics annoyed everyone. Three or four million pages of information on the testing of a new drug were submitted to the FDA. Step by step the agency reduced this mass of paper to a report of ten pages, and at last to a sentence or two. Did anyone involved in this process know all of what was going on? Was there anyone competent to say what relationship the final report bore to the facts? What were the facts, anyway, in those three million pages? Surely there couldn't be that many facts?

Yet it was obvious to Caitlin that coming to conclusions was a regular thing. It happened every day, and surprised no one.

Weren't the courts overburdened and the jails full?

Well, of course it would be very odd if everyone on the train was an old friend. The connections between people are thin, for the most part. You sat next to him on the 22 bus once, without knowing it. You wore the same color necktie on Tuesday. Your daughter was at school with someone of the same name. But it must be very rare for there to be serious competing explanations for a murder? Because his wife was running around, that's why. It's obvious. It's a damn love nest.

Perhaps it's a good thing it is so seldom necessary to inquire deeply into people's motives. In too many cases it would be impossible to say why people behave as they do.

The real mysteries, she supposed, have a random character. Because he was wearing a red tie.

A little girl disappears, her bicycle found in an irrigation ditch. If she hadn't stopped to pet the cat, if she hadn't been wearing a pink dress, if he hadn't decided to go instead by Priest Road, if he hadn't noticed that flash of pink—

Was there really any means of deciding the truth? But decisions had to be made nevertheless. That would account for the popularity of torture, at least, and the rarity of statesmen. But what did it mean then to be guilty? Is guilt only a measure of probability—that men with promiscuous wives are more likely to be thought guilty of something than those who wear red neckties? Are little girls guilty of something for wearing pink?

Perhaps that was where Crake went wrong. He had let himself be drawn into that way of thinking somehow, insensibly, over the years. Over the years of never being sure, of making do.

Statistical guilt. Guilt by association with the generally guilty class of men with promiscuous wives.

Caitlin ought to know something about that, being in the statistics business herself.

Ersatz guilt, because the real thing can't be had.

□

So Porres is living in the store, now?

Milo Crake, who rarely smoked, lit a cigarette for himself

from Tuchman's pack. The beat cop, just coming off duty, had looked in as he had been asked to and now found himself detained, waiting stiffly, while across the table the Lieutenant hunched over the ashtray, pinching a tender cigarette between flat fingers.

He's sleeping in the store, is that it?

He has a cot in the back room, Tuchman replied.

He's always had a cot in the back room.

I was told he hasn't been out all week.

Not out of the store. He must have a stove or something. What does he eat, I wonder? Has anyone looked in?

No sir.

His wife? Daughter?

Not to my knowledge. Would you like me to check the garbage?

Eh? What for?

To see what he eats.

God, no.

Crake looked up from his meditation but then, irritated by the officer's soft, innocent gaze, turned his back.

Old age is making you sarcastic, Frank.

I beg your pardon?

You can go. Thank you.

Tuchman slipped out. Too late, he remembered the pack of cigarettes left on the table.

□

James Porres closed the Mill Avenue Title Company at six o'clock as usual. Now he stood at the window, hands clasped behind his back, watching night fall in the street outside. It was Friday. The weekend alone lay ahead. The numbness in his body, which he seemed to inhabit through a television monitor, had not left him since the interview with Crake the Sunday before. He thought it was exhaustion.

Isela had gone, disappeared with Soccorro. So he had packed what he could carry on his bicycle and moved out too. He was pouting, he realized. Alone in the store at night, thinking over events since his partner's death, Porres had discovered and named self-indulgence. It was not exactly new country to him, but he had always before associated it with high mountains and grand panoramas. With those reckless things Bill had made his reputation on. His own particular, common and everyday self-indulgence was of the deserty kind: small, harsh, barren. His unprotesting acceptance of Isela's affair had been an indulgence of that sort. He had indulged himself in appearances: meekness, impotence, obstinacy. Chicken-necking, Isela called it. Fascism, was Soccorro's word. He had never thought much about Soccorro's complaint. Wasn't it just the usual adolescent struggling against her parents' will?

He considered the old Jewish ascetics, the desert patriarchs. Those were men he thought he understood.

How unlike herself, Caitlin thought. A contrast to her own extremity of self-doubt. The struggle with Crake must have brought that out in him: that sanctimonious moral assurance.

There had been a chicken-necking streak in Bill, too. A willingness to let other people believe what they liked about him. A little contempt for their views, perhaps. But she doubted he could ever have been accused of fascism, of using his spiritual wounds to manipulate people. He had been openly hostile to romanticisms of that sort: that saintliness must be anguished, that artists must be poor and struggling to find the depths of their souls. That's just a trick to excuse oppression, he had argued. To keep them poor and anguished and quiet. And then people wonder why they have a nihilist art and a punitive religion.

After that, she had not dared to criticize Bill's public personality.

Bill had always kept a kit in the store for emergencies—a cot, a Coleman stove, some pots and pans, blankets. That was his bohemian origin. He had nothing of Porres's ascetic inclination to hunker down, to retreat to the desert to harden his soul. It had only been a cache against The Bomb. Economic or spiritual thermonuclear destruction. He hadn't counted on being murdered, unless the gun counted.

The newly installed street lights came on. There was a certain tacky elegance, Porres admitted, to the reconstruction of Mill Avenue. The new shop fronts, the wrought iron benches and gas lamp reproductions, the brick paving, the interior courtyards with their miniature tile fountains and orange trees, all the artificial quaintness that Bill had wanted. And it was good for business. He wondered if it was a native style to anyone. Denver, with a sentimental Mexican influence. In twenty years it had spread everywhere, colonizing commerce like the English had colonized the nineteenth century. You wouldn't have thought that little island could mob the world so.

It was hard for him to sympathize with Isela. She had come apart. Suddenly come apart. But a mechanism which has run smoothly for forty years does not just fly apart. Perhaps it had not been running smoothly, after all. There must have been hidden wear, growing worse over the years until at last something jammed . . . The affair with Bill had kept her going so long, he supposed.

Soccorro had run off, too. What did that signify?

A cat was sitting in the street just under the awning of Woyke's shop opposite, watching him. Annoyed, Porres stepped back a bit into the shadow.

Only strangers can behave oddly, was his opinion. There is an internal logic to the strangest actions. What seems uncharacteristic only seems so from ignorance: anything can be explained, if necessary. One needs only time and sympathy.

It's no wonder human behavior is such a profound mystery.

For the first time in many years he felt an urge to smoke. He hadn't smoked since Soccorro was born, since the first reports of its danger. Soccorro had been a few days premature; she had surprised him before he had really quit. The numbness of nicotine withdrawal had helped him to get over it, actually. That was before men were thought to have an interest in childbirth. He had been impotent during Isela's pregnancy, crippled by a vision of thrusting too deep, releasing an amniotic flood, a blood tide. That was a source of friction between them for several years afterward. It had aroused Isela's contempt, he thought. Perhaps that was when she went to Bill?

He wished now that he had been allowed to help with the

birth. In the long unpleasant time afterward, when they were struggling to become a family, it would have helped if they had had that in common. He had had all sorts of fancies about childbirth. He had seen Isela lying naked in a pool of sauce, glistening like a fish in butter, screaming with the agony of penetration . . .

He hadn't thought of that in years. But he had kept his promise not to smoke, at least. He had never lacked for will, if there were something to attach it to. He was like the anemone that way.

Porres began to smoke when he was very young. The inclination of the larva to experiment, he supposed. It was an easy vice to acquire, more accessible than sex and alcohol, not so dangerous as stealing. To buy liquor required accomplices. His father had beaten him a little, half-heartedly, because of the tobacco, knowing how futile it was.

He remembered his father chiefly as a melancholy man of fragile moods who died at fifty-four of a heart attack and so was spared his old age, which would undoubtedly have been a sickly, graceless decline. Porres was inclined to regret his father. He supposed most men were. It was something to do with the breaking of authority. One regretted that, and regretted the weakness it revealed, and turned to religion.

These memories surprised him. He would have thought much of that had been drowned by now, like kittens.

He remembered one thing in particular: his father wakened at midnight by some boys knocking at his son's bedroom window. His father thick-lidded from sleep, stubbled, angry. As he bent over James's bed the shadow of a tree outside the bedroom window hid his face, and then a wind pushed the shadows momentarily aside. His father was accusing him of deception, complicity in secret crimes, to which he protested sleepy innocence. And then, for a brief instant, the moonlight illuminated him.

It's not true!

But his father did not believe him. Perhaps it was true, after all.

Across the street, Rufus Woyke came to the door of his shop and hissed at the cat, flicking his hand to drive it away. When it had gone he stood for a while in the open doorway, silhouetted by the light behind him, gazing across at the dark windows of James Porres, Antiquarian. Porres withdrew still farther into the shadow.

He had shopping and laundry to do. When he came out onto the street half an hour later Woyke's windows, too, were dark.

Not for many years, not since Woyke took over the trade and the occasional late hours, had Porres been downtown at night. Behind the restored area it was not much changed, he thought. Perhaps a little seedier.

The laundromat he remembered was in a small shopping center four or five blocks away, where there was also an all-night supermarket. Porres put his clothes into the washer, folded his paper laundry bag and laid it on top of the occupied machine, and crossed the parking lot to do his week's shopping. He had made a list, which was folded up now in his shirt pocket. The paper crackled pleasantly and he ran a finger down one sharp, neatly creased edge. Shopping for himself, this mundane task, produced an odd sensation. He had never been gregarious, but he had never lived really alone, either. Before his marriage there had been a few years in which he shared an apartment with Bill Face, and before that was childhood. Now he had stumbled out into the desert. He had been wandering, dazed, thirsty and sun-struck, and had come to this place—so familiar, yet threatening, its language unintelligible, its customs mysterious. A place, perhaps, which he had heard of for years and thought imaginary. Smaara . . .

Coming out of the market, instead of striking directly across the parking lot back to the laundromat, he kept to the lighted walk which ran along the store fronts. Ahead, halfway around, was the entrance to a theatre. At the box office, on the arm of some middle-aged man unknown to Porres, stood his daughter. For a moment the two of them were caught in the light of the marquee: the man bent forward anxiously, head to one side, as if peering into a tunnel, as if surprised like a rabbit in the glare of an oncoming auto. Soccorro's face was in shadow. She spoke briefly to the man as they passed inside.

Porres recovered after a long moment. He stepped forward,

intending to pursue them. Yes, he wanted a ticket. To which film?

There were three, and he was unable to decide.

Back in the laundromat, Porres removed his clothes to a dryer and sat down to wait, his bag of groceries beside him on the bench. On the bench opposite, with a similar paper bag, containing what seemed to be a black overcoat, sat one of the familiar Mill Avenue derelicts. Catching Porres's eye, he grinned and slowly lifted one hand in greeting. Porres stared rigidly forward.

How ya doin? Hey?

The man's voice was incongruously sweet, with the slightest burr. Porres frowned, and after a time the vagrant shuffled out.

But half an hour later, when Porres emerged with his groceries and his bag of laundered clothes, the man accosted him again, materializing out of the darkness behind the building.

How ya doin? Hey?

Porres ignored him and set off. It was a warm night, and with his arms full he soon began to sweat. Not wanting to walk up Mill, the lower end of which was garish with bars and surplus stores, he started up a side street. Here were run-down cottages on scruffy lots, the sidewalks overhung with unpruned citrus and littered with cast-off palm fronds. From open windows, invisible behind hedges of oleander and prickly pear, came sounds of jazz.

A good town for jazz, he had heard it said.

Just as he was about to stop and rest, the derelict appeared for a third time, out of an alley. So Porres did not stop, and the man scuffled along behind, enveloping Porres in his stench. The vagrant's soft, rotting voice tickled his ear.

How ya doin? Hey?

He seemed actually to want a reply to this mechanical question, but Porres only went forward a little more briskly.

Hey, scuse me, how ya doin? You jus go on there, it's OK, you don't hafta talk to me. Hoozat guy? Hey?

Porres's arms had begun to ache. The derelict continued to speak quietly at his back.

So your friend Bill's knocked in the head, hey? They asked

me about that one. I'll tell you a thing, hey. You jus go on there, mind your own business. Here's what, hey. They comes to me, so I says I seen em, this man and this flashy woman, bringing him in. They pull up back in Bill's car and carry him into the store, and in a little while the woman comes out and drives away. Who are they, hey? No idea, I says. What can you see in the dark, hey? Who wants to get so close? So what happened to the man, they want to know. He rides away on a bicycle, I says.

Porres stopped suddenly and turned on the man.

You lied, he snarled. The vagrant grinned and shifted his bag to the other arm.

How you know that, hey? What you know?

What cause do you have to tell lies about me? Porres advanced on him a step.

Hey, scuse me, how ya doin? This man's a friend of mine, Bill Face is. I know him from old times, hey? They going to come asking me what I know. What do I know?

So you told them lies. Why?

The derelict at last retreated a step.

Hey, you give em what they want. Who's going to believe me anyhow? I'm just tellin you, so's you know, hey?

The man took a few more steps backward and melted into the darkness. After some time, Porres took a deep breath and put his bags down on the walk. The spring air was suddenly very sweet. Porres gazed up into the sky, rubbing his aching arms, wondering what they had done to the vagrant to make him talk. Nothing, probably. Crake was too old to like unnecessary force.

There were no stars. It had been years since Porres had seen stars. The city sky was too bright for them.

Returning to the store, he let himself in the back. He put the bag of groceries and the laundry down on the cot in the work room and went forward through the darkened shop to look into the street. There was no sign of the derelict, but opposite, in Woyke's shop, a darker shadow moved and melted away. Porres returned to the back room and began to prepare supper.

Lies. What did he know?

When Porres had eaten he turned the light out and sat with his hands folded, listening. Then he got up and went up to the front again. Again the same shadow behind Woyke's window, melting away. Probably his own reflection.

Soccorro, he said to himself later, as he was falling asleep. Don't go with that man, he's too old for you. What do you want with him, love? You're too young, still too young . . .

Another week passed in this fashion. Then Porres became ill. The flu, he told himself. He shouldn't have been so miserly with his diet. He felt weak and sleepy. Perhaps it was the lack of exercise, now that he no longer rode his bicycle anywhere. On Saturday morning he was unable to get up and for the first time in years he did not open the store. There was nothing to eat, since he had been unable to go shopping. Fortunately, he had no appetite.

The weekend passed slowly. On Monday he felt no better. He woke before dawn, his mouth and eyes dry, and lay on his back staring up into the windowless darkness. He had eaten nothing for three days, but still did not feel particularly hungry. The grisly race between debility and disease would be soon decided: either he had already slept through the worst of it or another day would find him too feeble to help himself. Today he must get food. Suppose he collapsed in the street? He would be carried away somewhere for observation and never heard from again.

Some time later, what seemed to be mid-morning, he woke to find Luther Idge peering at him and axiously squeezing his shoulder so that it ached. It was the pain which wakened him. Clumsy fellow. What use did Woyke ever make of him? Porres had had several assistants, and had never liked any of them much . . .

Luther Idge was shaking him awake. What on earth did he want? Porres licked his lips several times before he could speak, and was surprised to find that he could only whisper.

Why are you here?

We were worried about you. You haven't opened since last week.

How did you get in?

With the key.

The key.

Can I get you something? Medicine?

Oh . . . What key?

Luther gaped at him, puzzled by this curiosity about keys when Porres, for all he knew, might be dying. Mr. Woyke's key, he said impatiently. Are you hungry? I could fix you something.

Yes, Porres whispered, levering himself up on one elbow. I am a bit hungry, I think. I've had the flu. Everything has been eaten. Will you go out? To the supermarket?

Sweat sprang out on his forehead and he fell back.

There is money, he said, gesturing toward the old wooden desk. Get bread, milk, eggs.

Luther pulled out several drawers and rummaged among the toiletries and spare shirts.

This? There's only three dollars.

Yes. That's enough.

Milk and eggs.

And bread. Not white bread.

Bread. Yes.

When Luther had gone, Porres closed his eyes. Woyke's key? He didn't remember Woyke having been given a key. Bill must have. What for? Porres fell into a doze and woke with a start as Luther returned with groceries which he put down on the folding table, next to the Coleman stove.

Boil the eggs, Porres directed. Three eggs.

Luther set to work pumping up the stove.

When the eggs were ready, Porres struggled to sit up. Luther gave him a plate with a slice of white bread on it. He was dizzy. The plate tipped and the bread slid onto the floor. At last, holding the plate on his lap, Porres broke one of the soft-boiled eggs so that it ran onto the bread.

I'm grateful to you, Porres said when he had finished the egg. His voice had returned. Luther, out of delicacy, had gone a little out of the room during the meal. There was no reply, and Porres's thoughts wandered for a moment before he took a second slice of bread and broke another egg over it.

Was it your idea to set a watch on me? Porres asked.

Mr. Woyke said I should, Luther replied. He had returned to stand in the doorway leading out into the store.

I owe him something for that, Porres muttered. As it happens. Though I shouldn't. For how long?

Since Mr. Face died.

That long.

Mr. Woyke said you mightn't like it.

No.

He thinks you ought to take some time off. Until this is all over. Close up the shop.

They won't let me.

No. I offered to look after the place, but Mr. Woyke said you mightn't like that.

They won't let me go away, I tell you.

No. But we ought to keep an eye on you, at least, Mr. Woyke said. So I did.

Thank you, Porres repeated. I'm grateful to you. He broke the third egg cleanly with the knife, feeling somewhat less dazed. And the question of the key was solved—it came to him then. Bill had talked about Porres's going away on vacation. Woyke was to look after the shop. He was to have a key for that purpose.

The shop remained closed on Monday. Late in the afternoon, Crake came poking around, peering in at the darkened window, trying the door. Porres watched with annoyance from the shadows.

On Monday evening he called home, wanting to talk to Soccorro. The telephone rang for a long time. Porres found it difficult to keep in mind that this sound, so empty and lonely, was only an electric current deliberately made audible by the machine in his hand in order to fill up the time, to reassure him that all was in working order. Ergonomics. No one answered, and he hung up finally.

Tuesday morning he felt well enough to open the store. He felt obliged to keep up appearances, though the legs trade had definitely fallen off since Bill's death. This street business had never amounted to much, anyway. Porres knew of dealers who dispensed with it entirely, whose only contact with strangers was mediated by the telephone and the mail. Now he could be freed even of that, by computer.

He hadn't yet found himself doing business with another dealer's computer, though. A conservative trade.

Crake returned at midmorning. For several minutes he scuffed about in the shop like a customer ill at ease among esoterica, hesitating to ask for only a copy of Graham Greene. This behavior, common in customers but unusual in Crake, made Porres immediately anxious. His mind became clouded, as by the rush from too large a mouthful of ice cream.

I have news, Crake said at last, approaching the desk where Porres sat dumbly waiting for the blow. But the blow did not come.

Yes? Porres choked, his throat dry.

Your daughter has killed herself.

Porres was aware of the detective's sudden, intense scrutiny, as if he expected in that moment to learn some fundamental truth. Porres did not stir. His hands were folded on the desk top, his head tipped to one side, his eyes on a pencil which lay on the blotter. A great many odd things went through his mind, as a man speared in the stomach might be startled by the novel sight of his entrails and wonder what he is to do with them on Friday next, when he is invited to a black tie dinner at the Senator's.

Crake went on speaking. She drove into the path of a ten-wheeler on the Black Canyon freeway, he said in a dry voice. She got on the wrong way at Bell Road, coming from the track.

From the track? What kind of people had she taken up with?

Definitely suicide, Crake was saying. She avoided a couple of little cars and tried to get in the way of a moving van before this. Very clean. No chance. The car was mashed flat.

Car. Her car?

The car, it seemed, belonged to a man named Dempsey. Left him stranded at the race track. Very upset. It was nothing to do with him, apparently. Picked her up in a bar once. Quite a fast little number. Forgot all about her until tonight. Remember me? she says. Wants to go to the track. Stayed one race and had to go back for her purse, or something. Borrowed the keys and took off. Little Japanese roller skate. Nothing left of it.

No, there wouldn't be. Why should there be?

Actually, he found out later, it was a Volkswagen. For a long time that seemed quite important.

Caitlin came in at lunch time. Porres was still sitting at his desk, hands in his lap.

I heard, she said. Porres raised his eyes.

I'm sorry, James.

Yes.

Later it seemed to Porres that she had had more to say, but he could not recall it. Probably he was rude. Crake, too, had been going on about something for a long while, sitting casually on a stool, his legs crossed, running his middle finger slowly up and down the crease of his trousers. What? Some theory of guilt, no doubt.

Porres rose at last, stiffly, and shuffled to the front of the store where he had spent so much of his time in the last few weeks. He gazed out into the street, which was nearly empty. The University was not in session.

Why on earth was Caitlin sorry? Well, that was the polite thing to say, wasn't it. Probably she really was sorry. Was she somehow to blame? Had she some part in this that he was ignorant of, an admission which Crake tried to extort from her by playing on her guilt? Had done so. It was Crake's idea that everyone was guilty, wasn't it? In some fashion. Unexceptionable, actually. Not always germane.

Across the street, Woyke was going home, leaving the store to Luther to lock up in an hour. Woyke turned up Mill in the direction of the number 60 bus stop. But then he saw Porres in the window and, deciding quickly, stepped into the street. Traffic was light. Woyke broke stride for a small truck and then, glancing at his watch, hesitated. The traffic light at the corner changed and a string of northbound cars marooned him on the safety island. While Woyke, standing in the middle of the street, watched anxiously over his shoulder for his bus, Porres locked the door and turned away. As he was turning on the light in the back room he heard Woyke rattle the knob once. Again. Then silence.

The back room was stuffy. Porres opened the door leading to the parking lot. A lizard, which had been cooling itself in a crack under the door jamb, skittered back onto the wall and froze, sitting up alertly.

Good afternoon, Porres said.

The lizard stared intently. It bore a slight resemblance to Woyke: the leathery folds of neck skin, the protruding mouth, the tiny eyes without whites.

I have done nothing, you know. Nothing. I realize, of course, that you have no eyebrows and cannot help staring.

The lizard raised its body away from the wall to which it clung and then flattened itself against the stucco again, rapidly, like the pumping of a piston. It was trying to obtain a perspective view, with a mechanical form of binocular vision.

A veritable detective.

Neither of them withdrew and so the confrontation continued.

The silence of lizards. Admirable. What would it take to break you, eh? Very hard. Very hard.

Porres extended his hand, slowly. The lizard disappeared.

□

That evening Isela came. Without knocking, she stepped in through the open back door. Porres was sitting on the cot, a cup of coffee and the stains of supper on a paper plate before him. Rising a little in surprise, he knocked against the table and spilled his coffee.

You heard?

Crake.

Isela's face seemed old to him. In two weeks he had already forgotten. Perhaps it was the lack of makeup?

How have you been? Isela said. Her voice was colorless. She was looking with some interest at the stock room where he had been living, and at the cot, he thought, with a little fondness, perhaps remembering some impromptu evening. She wore a gray suit, low heels, and kept a plain shoulder bag pressed close with one elbow. Was she a bit thinner? And her hair, worn loose in an unfamiliar way, was too long.

I'm all right.

She didn't come to see you?

Who?

S-Soccorro. Isela's voice trembled briefly before she brought it under control.

No.

There was no explanation, you know. I had no idea of what she'd planned.

No.

She seems to have planned it. So she told you nothing.

Nothing.

Why?

I imagine she was angry with me.

Intense irritation flashed in Isela's eyes. At once, they went dark again. How self-centered you are, she said.

Yes.

You should have reassured her.

How was I to do that?

Oh, your precious innocence, your good name. You let her imagine the worst.

Ah. Was I to acknowledge a lie, then?

Damn lies. Damn truth. It's your dignity at stake, isn't it?

Do you think it was my fault?

Isn't that what you think? Why couldn't you have done something for her? Why couldn't you have talked to her, instead of hiding here? What have you done? Nothing. Nothing!

There was a long silence, somewhat covered by the hissing of the water pipes as the automatic irrigation system for the potted plants in the gallery upstairs turned itself on. Isela had not come far into the room. For a brief moment Porres saw himself as a lizard and a wholly inappropriate giggle escaped him. But Isela was no longer looking at him and seemed not to notice.

It was just the same, she said at last, reflectively, when I wanted a second child.

Porres blinked, dumbfounded. When had she wanted a second child?

All you had to do then, Isela went on talking to herself, was to keep to yourself. All you had to do to prevent it was to mind your own business. And you did. You did.

Porres opened his mouth, gulping air like a fish.

This is how you get what you want. By doing nothing.

I, um—

Dammit. Dammit, dammit. If you would only give in you could have saved us all this!

She was trembling with rage. Then, in a blink, she was gone. The door slammed. A moment later he heard a car start at the mouth of the alley, grind into gear, buck, and stop. Again and again the car coughed, leaped, and died, until at last she got moving in a spray of gravel, rocks pinging against the other cars in the lot.

It had been quick, like a spark that leaves an acrid, burned taste in the air. Porres was better fitted for battles of attrition, for a long testing of arguments, a feeling for leverage. It was temperaments like Crake's that he was suited for, the lifelong clinch of marriage. He could stand up against that forever. But not a guerrilla who jumped out of hiding with a machine gun, firing indiscriminately.

Porres sighed and began to gather up his laundry. The homely chores would calm him. He had fallen behind anyway, during his illness.

Reluctant to go into the alley, he went out the front. Across the street, Luther Idge was standing in the doorway of Woyke's shop, talking to the beat cop. The police went on foot now, downtown, because of the vagrants. Woyke was staying open until nine o'clock. Stretching himself too thin. Not enough business to keep him, just enough to break him. Luther seemed to be saying something quite interesting. The patrolman was taking notes. Porres kept to the wall and got away without being noticed.

In the laundromat he was accosted again by the derelict who had seemed so sinister before. This time he was drunk.

Hey! How ya doin, my man?

The bum sat down on the bench beside Porres and leaned over confidentially. I heard the bad news, he said, a parody of condolence. Porres was briefly angry, but really was too tired for that. The drunken man kept on. It was on his conscience, he said, pulling a long face. He shouldn't have told them.

What can you do, hey? They wormed it outa me.

It was hard to tell whether his remorse was genuine. He seemed to be making an effort to overcome his intoxication, to speak with a distinctness he could not command even when sober. But the effort did nothing to dignify him, or to add gravity to his words. Remorse could do no more for him than Porres's innocence could cleanse him of guilt.

They musta got to her, the drunk was saying, over and over. They musta got to her. Jesus. What can you do, hey?

Porres closed his eyes and kept silence and after a while the wreck shuffled off, sniffling, leaving behind a morose, fetid smell.

Soccorro, don't go with that man, love.

It wasn't the same man, of course. What a lot of them there must have been. Why hadn't he known anything about it?

The silence of lizards.

□

Another week passed. He slept badly, harried by fragmented dreams, and woke before dawn, flushed and dry, tongue sticking to his lips. There were no more developments. He saw nothing of Crake; Isela kept to herself; Woyke continued to keep surreptitious watch.

Take some time off, Woyke had suggested. Close up for the summer. Get away from this.

Why did Woyke want him out of the way?

It was true that he could take care of business pretty well working two days out of the week. He had never liked keeping the shop open, but that was what Bill wanted. He would have to find a regular place to live soon, and then it would be just as easy to give up the store and run the business out of his home.

As the third weekend of his new life approached, Porres be-

gan to feel restless. His stomach, weakened by his illness, troubled him. He wanted some exercise. The narrowness of his new
routine bored him. On Saturday he closed the store and rode
through the neighborhood on his bicycle looking for a suitable
place to live. And then, invigorated, he began to think of an
expedition. Would it be possible to pedal all the way out into
the desert? Perhaps to the place where Soccorro took them,
not a month ago, for a picnic? Porres got out a map and was
disappointed to find that it was more than forty miles.

Were there other places nearer by? Studying the map, Porres
was surprised to discover how inaccessible the desert was to
someone without a car. He seemed to remember a time, not so
long ago, when it was possible to walk there. Was that true?
Perhaps because it was hot and dry, he had always assumed
that he lived in the desert. One saw these desert plants everywhere: saguaro, yucca, ocotillo, and the rest. But it was all artificial. This fierce, barren valley had been unable to support
even the tenacious Indians, the Hohokam with their engineering and their beans and their conservative ways. What would
happen without air conditioning and canal water?

Porres thought, on long reflection, that he used to see more
lizards about, before the bricks and the barn wood and the
automatic drip irrigation systems for potted plants.

Well, but all this would not make an expedition. He looked
at the map again. There was South Mountain Park, of course.
That was about fifteen miles.

Early on Sunday morning he set off. At dawn the streets
were quiet but already warm. The bicycle's tires hissed a little
on the softening tar. Perhaps he should have taken a hat?

The house on Greenway Drive was dark, Isela still asleep. For
a moment Porres thought of taking the car, but his anticipation
of an adventure was too strong. The city where he had lived un-
thinkingly for so long appeared suddenly exotic to him. James
Porres, dealer in rare works of travel and exploration, had never
liked the exotic much. Before now.

Through the silent suburban developments he rode with his
head down, his thoughts elsewhere. Held up by the traffic light
on 56th, he stopped to take stock. The park was long and nar-

row, just part of the ridge of a pocket mountain range that
bounded the valley on the southwest. The near end of the park
was hardly a mile away, but the park entrance was ten miles
down Baseline Road. Wasn't it possible to get in a back way?
Through the resort, perhaps, or the suburbs to the south? Why
hadn't he brought the map? He had never ridden any distance
by bicycle. Travel by bicycle changed his whole mental geogra-
phy entirely out of recognition.

Porres decided to bear south on 56th, which soon was re-
named the Avenida del Yaqui and he found himself in a strange
place, an Indian and Chicano town. He rode slowly down the
main street, amazed. No one was about. Intensely picturesque
buildings—a tiny whitewashed church, a tumbledown cantina—
stood between shacks which seemed to be made of scrap wood,
with here and there a frame cottage half painted pink. There
were no sidewalks; there was no vestige of landscaping. The
buildings seemed to be simply lying on the bare ground, as if
everything but the church might be blown away in the next
dust storm. Nothing grew but native cactus and salt bush,
plants of a dusty green, almost gray color.

The strangeness of this, its sudden discovery, shocked him.

Yet when he looked carefully he saw familiar things. There
was poverty, certainly. There were also televisions and air con-
ditioners and little plots of petunias by the door.

Bewildered, he got off his bicycle in the middle of the street.
Off to the west the mountain rose up, its flanks still moss-green
from the winter rain, and running up the ridge was a jeep track.
But Porres had forgotten about the freeway which here separated him from the park. He turned around, and in twenty minutes was back on Baseline Road. The K-Mart and the pancake
restaurant, the rosemary-covered slopes of the entrance to the
industrial park, all seemed just as peculiar and mysterious, and
for a moment Porres was disoriented.

He set off down Baseline toward the park entrance, passed
under the freeway, and rode through orange groves as far as
40th Street before stopping again to reconsider. Here the High-
line Canal passed under the road. He could turn off onto the
towpath on the south side of the canal. Perhaps an opportunity

would arise of getting into the park that way.

But none did. He rode slowly through the morning heat, turning off now and then to explore streets which always came to a dead end, blocked by chain link fences. By noon he reached the park entrance road, where he stopped to rest in the shade of a cottonwood growing on waste ground beside the canal. He hadn't thought to bring water. The top of his head felt a little sunburned. He was discouraged.

Porres had no real experience of the desert, and was beginning to realize what an insulated life he had led. The accusations which Isela made were true enough. And what had he known of Soccorro, before now? Nothing, it seemed. Innocence has two aspects. That was as bitter a notion as had ever come to him.

Everything has two aspects. Doesn't it?

Porres thought that when he was younger the desert was more grand, that it was more of an adversary. The canyons of the Superstitions were full of hermits then, before it was made an official wilderness, and everywhere the desert was worn bare with mine holes and waste, the grass gone to grazing. Now, he was told, the hermits were gone, the bush was grown up lush, and all that remained—the mine refuse, the broken rock and the pits scrabbled in the hard clay—was actually restoration. Atmosphere.

But it was still possible to die in there, in the summertime, almost within sight of office buildings. It happened every few years. So there were still irreparable mistakes, still things one would not be forgiven.

From the safety of shade, Porres gazed out over the scoured scrub land along the canal. A creosote bush growing twenty yards away was the only substantial plant which shared this plot with the cottonwood under which he sat. That was an oddity in itself, creosote and cottonwood together, and it looked odd even to an uneducated eye. The tan earth was rimed with white streaks of salt.

It was a barrenness quite artificial.

Was this actually the desert? Perhaps he hadn't reached the desert yet.

Porres stood up. Wearily, he walked with his bicycle to the road. He would go as far as the park entrance itself, a mile or so more, and turn around. Like Moses at the gates of Canaan. Smiling at the effrontery of this idea, he mounted his bicycle and began at last to pedal up the mountain.

□

Rufus Woyke's case came to trial at the end of October. Caitlin went to watch, but it actually amounted to very little. The arguments of the prosecution were just what she had worked out for herself and the motion of the defense for dismissal was granted. The evidence was, indeed, entirely suppositious.

Woyke did not look particularly healthy. He had always been sallow, but now his flesh had a soft, waxy appearance that was very unpleasant. He paid hardly any attention to the proceedings, which were no danger to him in any case, and never spoke to his lawyer. Sometimes he looked vaguely in the direction of the person giving testimony, as if wondering how the witness could find so much to say. He had a sack of pink mints in his pocket which he dipped into every fifteen minutes or so. By three o'clock it was all over and Woyke was led away, returned to prison to continue serving his sentence.

Caitlin made a few inquiries afterwards, and the next day a telephone call. One day in mid-November she drove out to the penitentiary at Florence to visit the prisoner Woyke.

On the Gila River reservation the cotton crop was beginning to be harvested, which meant first killing the plants with a defoliant and leaving them to dry, so that with an overcast sky the desert now looked particularly bleak. Some fields were already trampled and broken; in others the brown shrubs were still spotted with pallid fluffs of cotton looking more like mold. Behind everything rose stark mountains of gray slag. Bins of picked cotton sat under tarps at the edges of the fields and machinery was parked under metal shelters, but there was no one at work. Caitlin didn't think she had ever seen anyone at work on these big-time farms. There were no houses or barns. Orientals don't live on their farms, either. The Oriental style on a giant scale.

111

The prison at Florence looked just as it did in all the movies that had been made there: stucco and concrete blocks piled up at the base of a square tower and surrounded by bare, cleared desert. The buildings were too squat, the windows too small, to pass for anything but a prison even without the other trappings. Tiny windows, she discovered, were more ominous than no windows at all. That was why it was so often in the movies, because here the appearance of a penitentiary was brought to perfection.

Penitence.

There was still the question of whether Woyke would see her, which she could only test by making the attempt. Caitlin was herded into the visitors' room with the others, all women, and left to wait on the bench which divided the big hollow room in two. She dried her hands nervously with a tissue. The others all seemed to know each other. They chattered in a mixture of Spanish and English, tossing their heads and making incomprehensible jokes about the la-la white woman in the lawyering clothes. The men, too, when they were brought in, were curious about her, and glanced covertly down the row.

Woyke had come, and took his seat opposite, puzzled but too indifferent to want an explanation. He waited heavily, saying nothing. But Caitlin did not intend to waste her few minutes in politeness. She began briskly.

Did he know her?

He allowed it.

She explained her business, her unofficial standing. Was he willing to talk about Bill Face?

He might be.

What exactly was the connection between you? Was it blackmail?

A spark of resentment gave brief life to his voice and he asked with irritation what concern that was of hers.

It was no concern of hers whatsoever. She was, quite brazenly, meddling.

Woyke was obviously nonplussed at such a frank answer. Six months in jail had increased his reserve to the point of absurdity. Caitlin shrewdly guessed that his reticence would be mostly on the small everyday matters for which he cared nothing, so that indeed he spoke not at all for days on end, until some large subject would be broached and he jabbered away unconsciously, a little uncomfortable, as if he suspected his fly were open. And afterward he would think back, wondering uneasily if he had been indiscreet. He had become completely transparent, imagining all the while that taciturnity made him opaque. Jail life had made him eccentric, but had mercifully withheld self-knowledge. Driving home again after the interview, Caitlin thought it would be odd if an experienced interrogator like Crake had been unable to get anything out of Woyke, when an amateur like Caitlin had done well enough.

She was still not breaking trail. If Crake had known all this, why had he continued to pursue Porres so fiercely?

Woyke had not been strictly truthful, of course. Was anyone? But what he said accorded so well with Caitlin's own idea of Bill's character that she instinctively believed him. But later, ruefully: on that ground alone she ought not to have.

Anything which fits one's views too well is probably false. How on earth would crimes ever be solved if the police thought like that? It was a good thing detectives were not particularly metaphysical, she thought, or the public would never be permitted any illusion of justice at all.

In the course of six months of casual inquiries, Caitlin had discovered nothing at all about Bill's death, but a good deal about some things she had always taken for granted. She was an accountant by temperament as well as training, inclined to a view of truth as a fact no more obscure than a balance sheet, always visible to the sufficiently sharp-sighted. The obstacles to knowledge, it seemed once, were laziness and a lack of information. There were practical difficulties, certainly. Perhaps no one would ever understand the finances of a company like IBM when so many had labored so long to make them unintelligible. Such a problem made one tired. Knowledge wasn't worth it.

But then she had gone on into economics. Here the behavior of a great many little unpredictable parts yielded an aggregate enticingly simple. One did not need to know, after all, the position of every atom to know where the stone was lying. And

yet, it seemed that whenever she reached out for it, her hand
closed on nothing, as if she had tried to pick up a reflection
from the bottom of a pond, and then the mud roiled up and
obscured everything for a while.

Luther Idge had a lurid imagination which naturally exagger-
ated the dark dealings which everyone was so eager to attribute
to Bill. Woyke just as naturally did the opposite, flattening
everything out in mundane sunlight. Caitlin found the mundane view the more comfortable. She was certain that Bill
would never have submitted to open blackmail, but his soft
heart might have suggested a charity which his hard head would
recognize at once as prudent, and so it would be done. Bill
Face never talked about his motives. Woyke had cynically assumed that it had been done to keep him quiet.

But it was never discussed between you at all?

No.

Now Caitlin was nonplussed. Could it really be all a house of
cards? What did Woyke know that he thought was so important?

But Woyke headed off elliptically. He could never understand, he said, what Bill saw in Isela Porres. He simply couldn't
help himself, of course. What a frosty woman. All sensible people are selfish.

Now that Caitlin had gotten him started, Woyke went on
under his own power, talking disconnectedly of this and that.
He was a genuine eccentric, crazy enough to be a scapegoat, not
crazy enough to be afraid of. That protected him from a good
deal of prison violence, no doubt. If he had been really crazy,
grandiosely insane, he might have been spared some reverence at
the cost of his life.

Time was called. Woyke was taken away, a stooped and fifty-
ish man in a baggy cotton shirt and colorless overalls.

She wondered what on earth he could have been like as a
young man, when he and Bill first met. A dreamy-eyed poetical
youth, peddling dope to children? An oaf? A sharp kid with a
glass jaw?

Caitlin drove home, her mind at loose ends. The air was perfectly clear for the first time in months, the disorienting clarity

that magnifies distant landmarks and confuses perspective. She was tired. On impulse, on a stretch of road where it took a long curve to the west around some isolated mountain, she stopped the car and got out.

The desert had always exhilarated her, probably much more than someone native to it. She had grown up in Michigan, had come here to school. She had never thought the desert bleak, or hostile in the way that appeals to eremites. It was exotic, majestic, grand. Palm trees and saguaro against a sunset sky, honey-colored desert grass rippling under a hot wind, a hillside upholstered in a thousand shades of gray and green, a wilderness of twisted red canyons overlooked by a black mesa, a distant cottonwood silvered by the sun, standing alone against a shadowed cliff threaded by a waterfall that died before it reached bottom—such things provoked a silly and sentimental response in her which she had given up resisting. It was a harsh, killing place as well as beautiful. The wind that sprang up before a dust storm, fiercely hot, out of a dark brown sky, put her in a religious panic that as the child of a benign Ypsilanti doctor she had never known.

The long desert summer was now over. Caitlin walked out some distance to a little rise where she sat down, after inspecting the bushes for snakes. Away to the north, a faint pall on the horizon marked the city's eastern suburbs. In the middle distance an Air Force transport lumbered in from the west, too far away to be heard. It was pleasant to be here, to reassure herself that there were still things for which she had no importance, that the whole earth had not yet shrunk to the measure of man.

Bill's feelings would have been quite the opposite, she felt certain. Everything he had valued would vanish in the desert. He had lived every minute of his life in the midst of civilization, and had thought no more about that than he would of going for a constitutional on the bottom of the ocean. Caitlin could not imagine what had held Bill and James Porres together for so many years. Porres was not an especially sympathetic man. He possessed something which insulated him from the great passions. If he had had Somerset Maugham's objective interest in everything under the sun, that aloof, immoral curiosity which made his books so annoying to Caitlin, Porres might have done something quite astonishing. As it was, he was just a cold fish. As cold as Bill had been hot.

Caitlin lacked the cosmopolitan ability that Bill had had to empathize with anyone. She lacked that extremity of self-confidence that had permitted Bill to lay himself out so graciously without fear of being trampled on. She did not think of herself as suspicious or stingy, but she had never liked to stand comparison with Bill. And he had not been soft. He had been like an old apple: firm, loose-jacketed, fragrant.

Both Isela and the Lieutenant had laughed in Caitlin's face. They thought her feelings about Bill were sighing and naive.

Bill hadn't had any principles, she saw now, other than pleasure and the preservation of his own freedom. If his actions were on the whole admirable, Caitlin knew now that it was an accident—because, having money and power, it was easier for him to be accommodating and charitable. If he had had a vicious streak people might have found him more understandable, if not predictable.

What *had* Bill seen in Isela Porres? Woyke had been mystified: the only thing which could touch his imagination was a grand passion. Isela was certainly capable of that, but Bill would never have put up with the trouble. Perhaps he hadn't seen anything at all in her. Perhaps he hadn't thought it necessary to do so merely in order to conduct an affair. That was a typically male attitude, wasn't it? Caitlin wondered how true it was. She had never felt very capable of love, herself. She doubted whether she had ever met anyone with much of a talent for it. Probably the scarceness of love accounted for its importance in people's minds. It would be too bad, she thought, if love were never to be confused with sexual infatuation, or hunger for security, or any of the other needs that drove couples together. We would all live more hard-bitten and unfucked lives in that case.

What had Porres known of Bill? Caitlin had developed a shrewd if somewhat prejudiced idea of Porres as the sort of sanctimonious person who is perfectly familiar with dirt but, because of some constipation in the subconscious, never seems to learn anything about it. He was the kind of man who could do a murder with the left hand, as it were, by a little adjustment here and there, not noticing. Nothing so crude as arsenic in the Cremora.

Crake had had that tested, surely?

Abruptly, Caitlin laughed. What was she doing but finding reasons to dislike an uncongenial person? Actually, he hadn't always been so uncongenial. Events had exposed his weakness, changed him. Caitlin hoped she would never be unlucky that way, herself.

It was true, though, that Porres was singularly blind to what went on around him. What in other people would have to be called callousness or bigotry was, in Porres, merely ignorance. And Bill had encouraged this, apparently. He had gone out of his way to protect Porres from the truth. That seemed to be the burden of what Woyke knew, and the source of Woyke's imaginary power over Bill. With a start, Caitlin realized she may have witnessed all these years a species of love. After all.

She remembered the instance of the black poetess whose book the shop agreed to publish. Porres had bungled it. The manuscript was destroyed. Bill took the loss and the blame.

Of course, there was more to it than that. There was the notorious shouting match on Mill Avenue. You could at least visit the child, the woman had screamed hysterically at Bill's retreating back.

Dammit, Bill, you might at least have thought what harm it will do the business. Can't we go ahead and publish the book in spite of this? It will look more as if you meant well.

No, James, the book is lost.

Porres clapped his hands with irritation. So she won't let us have it now? It's no wonder.

No, James. Lost.

What? Mislaid?

Bill crossed his long legs, shrugged, stared at his fingers' ends.

Dammit Bill—

Caitlin imagined them as she had seen them so often. Bill sat folded up on a little stool beside the coffee pot, his elbow resting on the table, the ever-present cup of coffee in his hand. Porres paced impatiently in a half-circle around the desk or stopped to browbeat his much taller partner who sat so complacently, abashed, on a footstool.

Indeed, as Woyke justly observed, a very small knowledge of Bill's crimes would have been enough to break Porres's brittle trust. And no one but Bill would have cared.

The sun was halfway down in the west. A cold breeze stirred up a little dust devil which gave Caitlin a momentary shiver and then whirled away downhill and across the road.

A good-sized prickly pear was growing beside her, one last withered purple fruit clinging to the edge of an upper pad. A lizard sunned itself on the ground, within cautious reach of the protection of the cactus. Caitlin stirred, stiff from sitting motionless for so long. The lizard did a few quick pushups, decided it was not safe, and vanished.

Caitlin stood up and reached for the cactus fruit. It had spines, but not so close together as the young pad to which it clung, and she twisted it off without sticking herself too badly. The real problem was the small clusters of hairs called glochids, which she scraped off with the edge of a stone before biting into the fruit. It was dry and woody, but had a subtle perfumed sweetness that saved it from insipidity.

The ubiquitous lizard ventured out into the sun again.

A little late in the season for you, isn't it?

The lizard cocked its head. Caitlin walked back down to her car.

Woyke would be let out in another six months or so, she supposed, unless someone contrived to blame him for something else. What would he do then, with his livelihood gone? Well, what had he done before? She didn't know. And it hadn't been much of a living, apparently. He would contrive to get by, no doubt, as he had always done.

Caitlin was tired of this unprofitable business. As tired as Crake himself must have been, at the end.

□

One afternoon about a month after Bill Face's death Crake stopped Caitlin on the street as she was leaving work.

Another cross-examination? Caitlin slipped on her mirrored sunglasses and put her purse between them.

A small one, Crake admitted, smiling.

Aren't you busy? Do you know where all your criminals are?

Crake bobbed his head. He wanted a few minutes, somewhere free of interruption, where she wouldn't get away before he was finished. Over dinner, let's say.

I'd say dinner was the least you owed me, she replied at once. You must take me somewhere decently expensive.

He named a restaurant within walking distance, an adobe house converted into a dark, cool nest of tiny, nearly private dining rooms with heavy black wooden furniture and uneven floors. She ordered a pitcher of margaritas and the most costly thing on the menu.

Crake drank sparingly. I like to keep the upper hand, he explained.

They talked about other things until the food was served: about the last time there was water in the river, and the effect of weather on violent crime, and that eucalyptus trees had finally been put into the empty planters on Mill Avenue.

There will be shade in ten years, Caitlin said, opening her napkin.

Very pleasant for someone.

Crake took a pair of reading glasses from his shirt pocket and put them on before taking up his silverware. With a surgical air he pared a very thin slice from his steak and chewed it slowly, gazing at Caitlin over the top of his glasses.

We had to rescue your Mr. Porres yesterday. He went for a bicycle ride without water. We found him walking up to the entrance of South Mountain Park with the beginnings of heat exhaustion. One of my men took him home in the back of a truck.

How foolish of him. Why do you say he belongs to me?

Crake put down his knife and took off his glasses. He wasn't at all hungry. Resting his thick forearms on the table, he leaned forward and stared rudely at Caitlin.

You're a silly little drink of water, Caitlin.

That's offensive, Lieutenant.

Yes, isn't it? But: you're bright. I want that gun. I want to know who it belonged to, and what it was for, and where it is now. I want to know what you know about this. Your Mr. Porres says he's never heard of a gun in the shop. He's never heard of Bill Face keeping a gun.

Entirely uncharacteristic of him.

Crake smacked his palm on the table. Then where did it come from?

Caitlin shrugged. She picked up the glass which had been overturned and wiped up a bit of wine on the table. She pushed her plate aside.

There was never a gun kept there in my time, she said. It would certainly not have been kept on the shelf, but in the desk drawer with the flashlight, where it could have been got at. I never heard of it before this. The most that can be said for it is that anyone stupid enough to point a gun at Bill should have been prepared to use it.

That seems not to have been necessary, Crake observed.

Yes. What *did* Bill die of?

Lieutenant Crake smiled and ignored the question. We were speaking of the gun, he said, with emphasis. Now my first idea was this: the job was done by someone who came in with him. There was a conversation between them, eh? Coffee for Bill. Business. He contrives to get some books down from the top shelf. That was the reason for coming to the store in the first place, I imagine, to get what was there on the shelf, behind the books. But the reason was guessed. This doesn't explain, of course, why the books were put back so oddly. And it doesn't explain why the flashlight batteries were dead.

Isn't it likely that the flashlight was lying on the floor all night?

No. Why clear up the books and not the flashlight? Such a suggestive natural detail.

But there was one book.

Yes. He was still holding it. To take it wouldn't have been safe.

It was on the floor.

Yes, that was Porres's doing.

Oh, he would have wanted to see what it was, wouldn't he? Just like him to look at it without thinking.

Mm. Now. Let's suppose instead the job is done this way: by someone who lies in wait, on a night when Bill is expected. Using the flashlight, you see.

Yes. What use would Bill have had for it? He would have just turned on the light, wouldn't he, in his own place.

So. Face shows up as expected. But he's brought a woman. Left her in the car. Now what? Can't shoot him and get away without being seen. Improvise. The woman gets tired of waiting, comes in to find out what's taking so long. Bill's had an accident. She makes herself scarce and the guilty party slips out.

Will you find the waiter? I want some coffee.

The question is, Crake went on, ignoring her request. After slipping out, why does he come back?

Could I have some coffee?

The blood. Several hours later, to bloody a corner of the desk. To pick up a little, put the flashlight away, remove the gun. Improve appearances. Not too much.

Yes, she thought. Everything is explained away, but nothing is explained. The books reshelved so awkwardly, the cat's blood and the coming and going in the car. Why manufacture evidence which points nowhere? Why take the chance of coming back?

But if it were no chance: if it were Porres? Why should he not be in the shop at opening time, cleaning up? Not too much cleaning up of course. Dangerous to be too clean. Just enough to muddle things. There would be some heat, of course. Some scrutiny. He could stand that, if he kept his mouth shut.

Who was the woman, then? If it were Soccorro: if it were her father and not Woyke who drove her home in Bill's car. Then Soccorro had known.

But no. It was she, Caitlin, who was the woman in the case. Crake kept her well into the evening. He made no accusations. He said nothing at all that was clearly the truth, but spun out one new explanation after another, plausible but shabby and unsatisfying explanations.   She recalled a production of *The Merchant of Venice*, with Shylock as a victim of anti-Semitism. It had really been quite plausible, quite horrifying.   She had fallen entirely into sympathy with the poor unshriven banker. But the play was transformed from a comedy to a lugubrious tragedy that sat on her stomach like unrisen bread. The evil in it was no longer Shylock's; it was no longer on purpose, or coldly, or for the hell of it, but only the bumbling of a pack of bigots, kidnappers, con artists, and ignorant apostates. The original Shylock could never have been extenuated that way. But there was no good in the modern moral bleakness, either. The new Shylock was a punitive miser set upon by rednecks.

She had hated it. It was exactly her vision of good and evil, realized on the stage, and she had hated it.

Perhaps, like the desert, life could become so barren that it became grand?

She thought of Porres, lying in wait, surprised by his own daughter.

Surely he couldn't have planned it all? Surely that, at least, was a surprise.

□

Milo Crake was having difficulty sleeping. He would go for a drive on a hot night and invariably end by keeping watch from his parked car on the Porres house, or the bookshop, or some other focus of his obsession.   After dinner with Caitlin he walked slowly down Mill Avenue to take up his familiar position across the street from the bookshop, in the shadows of the entrance to the inner mall. He leaned against the iron gate which at night blocked the passage down into the plaza, an enclosed warren of little shops and a good place for a rape.

A warm breeze smelling of beer and motor oil swirled through the street and died. Crake shifted his feet after an hour or so, to relieve his knees.

The Vachon woman had been dangerous. He had wanted to be sure of her, to be sure she could not be forced into the part he had worked out for Soccorro Porres. But she had defended herself too well. Her arguments had threatened his own case.

Fast on her feet, the bitch.

It hadn't been a hard case, actually. The Captain was going to have something to say about personal involvement, no doubt, and delegation of authority. But they would buy it, the prosecutor and the captain. It was sellable.

If only it were a little flashier. Crake thought he would have liked to get hold of something by the big end one time.

When he was young, Crake had had a little facility for drawing, and had once thought of a career in art. Nothing so ambitious as a painter, of course. Cartooning. Or drawing newspaper advertisements for department stores. The summer after graduating from high school he went to New York for the first time, with his parents. In the war he was an MP.

Everybody, he supposed, had such experiences.

Probably the way to be happy was to get laid regularly.

□

The following afternoon, a Friday, Milo Crake sat in the Captain's office making the usual, obligatory report. The Captain, a thin man meticulously dressed, was tapping a pencil against his thumbnail. The faint, inexorable tapping was the only sound, the only sign of his irritation.

It's not much of a case, Milo, he said at last, turning to face his Lieutenant.

No, sir. It's difficult that way.

Who is under surveillance now?

James Porres.

Ah. Well, more surveillance isn't justified, I suppose. The Captain paused to reflect before continuing. He began to doodle, speaking slowly. A strategem to bring the gun out of hiding would have to rest on a bit firmer ground than we have now, I think. Otherwise it might backfire, mightn't it? We would be accused of trying to manufacture evidence. I think I will have to oppose that idea, Milo.

Yes, sir.

Ah. That will be the end of the business with the gun, I

think. Now don't you think, Milo, that if this person was simply tidying up, shall we say, he would have come forward by now?

If it was an accident, yes.

Mm. But of course, he might not be certain of that. He might think he was in danger of being accused of something more serious.

I'd rather not pull back now, Crake interjected, seeing the Captain's thinking.

Oh, I agree. If we pull back, hoping to draw the man in that way, it would be quite difficult to reactivate the case without new evidence. Considering the thinness of it, you know. I doubt if I could justify the expense. And the probability of new evidence is very low.

Crake nodded, shifting uncomfortably in his chair. This case was always left for last, and he had been sitting for over an hour in the Captain's office. He was beginning to fear he would not get out in time to catch Tuchman. He should have left a message with the duty officer. Meanwhile, the Captain went slowly on thinking out loud.

There is a woman involved. A witness?

Easily discredited. A street person, he added delicately.

Ah. That's out, then.

The woman is dead, sir. Suicide.

Is she? Well.

What about putting Rufus Woyke under surveillance?

No, I don't think we can justify that, can we?

The Captain stood up and walked across to the window, which looked north toward the butte that rose up behind the football stadium a few blocks away. After a bit he rocked back on his heels, usually a sign that the conference would be over shortly. At last he turned and sat on the narrow sill, gripping it with his hands and stretching out his long legs, his pale boots elegant against the chocolate rug. Crake, still sitting beside the Captain's desk, had half turned to look over the back of the chair.

I hate to be involved in this, Milo, the Captain said. It should have been handled lower down.

Yes, sir.

If the matter had been wrapped up quickly there would have been no questions asked. However. Bill Face was a prominent enough man to justify your actions, I imagine.

That was all. Crake rose and crossed the soundless carpet to the door. The latch drew back with a liquid snick, the sound of a cartridge clip in a pistol. Then he was through, and let the door drift closed by itself as he set off down tht hall to the duty room. Tuchman was straightening his hat by his reflection in the mirrored front of a soda machine. Crake paused in the doorway to watch.

The patrolman was young, still in his twenties, still in baby fat. He looked like a store clerk or a teacher, despite the uniform—like someone who does not expect to be listened to carefully. It was the eyes. Crake thought he had met Tuchman's wife at a PBA dance. A redhead. They wanted them with wives and kids now. Family men. Made them less reckless. Also hard to schedule. Crake realized that he didn't know the patrolman's first name. Was it Frank?

He stepped forward into the room. Tuchman straightened and turned.

You're going out, Frank? I'll walk with you.

The two of them ambled away toward the parking lot without speaking. Tuchman, uncomfortable with his superior walking behind, hung back a little and received a slight nudge. They reached the patrol car.

I'm detaching you for the weekend, Frank. Unofficially, you understand. The Captain won't allow any additional men on the Face murder.

Tuchman shuffled uneasily, and his transparent eyes crinkled with annoyance.

Plans, Frank?

I was going to take the kids up to Canyon Lake. Bass fishing.

Oh? How old?

Four and five. The boy's seven.

Seven? Good Christ. The man must be almost thirty, then, and just starting out. Ought to get out his file. Four years as a military librarian, degree in accounting, that sort of thing. Used to get them out of high school, ready to stuff your ass in a sack. What happens to the tough boys now? Innocents, ripe for picking, left on the tree to rot until the wind brings them down? Windfall fruit, to a Pennsylvania mountain boy. Fruit in the desert is a springtime produce. After the rain. Cholla chains, saguaro apples. Lumpy, tubercular things, with prickles that crawl up your arm like ants. Mesquite. It was all mesquite to him: some leathery bush with pods of beans like gravel. Tuchman's wife would make jelly out of it. Mesquite jelly. Cactus jelly.

Put it off, Frank.

Yes sir.

The patrolman was tall, with a deep soft voice. A good man for investigating rest home murders.

We're going to have a break in this case, Frank. I want to keep on top of it. In an hour or so I'll be going around to speak to Rufus Woyke. Give him a little advice. You'll tell me what happens afterward.

Yes sir. I shouldn't be in uniform, then?

This is unofficial, Frank. No one knows I've ordered extra surveillance. It's your beat, you're expected to be there. Stick to your beat, keep an eye on Woyke's shop, and report to me tomorrow morning.

Punks, Crake thought when Tuchman had driven away. What the hell happens to the kids who used to grow into punks? Quit making em.

He walked across the lot to his own car, parked in the shade on the north side of the building. It was an old Volvo sedan, without air conditioning. Four o'clock. He turned the radio to the local talk station, hoping for a weather report. Someone said it had broken a hundred degrees. He hoped so. He'd put twenty dollars into the pool on today.

Lieutenant Crake lived in a townhouse apartment, leased, on a cul-de-sac behind a discount department store. About the time he moved in someone planted a little queen palm beside the walk, which had since grown so that it blocked the gate. Now a path had been worn around to a hole in the fence, he saw. The people in the first unit. Crake seldom parked in the front, himself, but in the covered parking at the rear.

It was stuffy inside. He left the front door standing open for light and crossed the living room to a credenza piled up with magazines and video game cartridges. In the corner, on top of the television, the green emerald eye of the videotape monitor glowed in the darkness. He'd forgotten what it was set for. In the back of the credenza, behind some rolls of Christmas wrapping, extra tablecloths, a box of candles, and other miscellany, he kept a spare gun swaddled in a pillowcase. It was a long time since he'd had it out. Not since he moved here. The gun was something he'd picked up after a bust in the sixties. A .38, similar to a police revolver. In those days it was thought to be a good idea to carry an extra gun sometimes, one that couldn't be traced back to you. He'd never needed it. The idea had seemed a little gamey, actually, and after a while he put the thing away and nearly forgot about it. Hysterical times, those. But it would be just as well, he thought, to be on the safe side if he were going to pop a cork. In case the bottle broke. Like a waiter with a towel around his hand.

He sat down on the edge of the sofa, unwrapped the gun, and set to wiping it clean with the pillowcase.

The place should be aired out, he thought. It seemed as if he were never home any more, since the Face killing. You don't know what you smell like until you come back home after an absence. He smiled, remembering frantic efforts as a kid to learn whether his breath smelled of cigarette smoke.

The room was hot and close. He was sweating. Finished, he wrapped up the gun again, carefully, and laid it on the coffee table. Somewhere in the pile of magazines on the credenza was a television schedule. The video recorder, he found, was set for a game show he had never heard of. He turned it off.

Crake wanted to catch Woyke as he was closing up and would be anxious to go home. There was easily half an hour yet. He got a cold frankfurter out of the refrigerator and poured himself a glass of iced tea. Spreading the newspaper out on the counter, he studied the comics and chewed slowly on the frankfurter. Then he took the glass of tea and went to stand outside on the front step, where it was cooler.

He was going to shake things up. It would be just as well if
there were some inconsequential thing he could take a rap for,
if things went bad. Unauthorized surveillance would do. Something that was never objected to ordinarily.

Rufus Woyke was, at this stage, almost as plausible a suspect
as Porres. He had the means and could be supplied with a motive. The motive, however, would be trivial in comparison, and
therein lay the weakness of any case against Woyke: it had no
grandeur. It was mean and little. And Woyke was such a suspicious, grudging man. What did he fear from Porres that he
should keep so close an eye on him? Setting his shop boy Idge
to watch like that. Well, that could all be turned against him.
He could be used to get at Porres.

When he had finished his tea, Crake set the glass down just
inside the door, picked up the gun from the coffee table, and
locked up. The drive back downtown took twenty minutes in
rush traffic. It was a quarter past five when he parked on a side
street back of Mill. Tuchman was in place, the squad car parked
on the corner. Crake walked quickly down the street to the
bookshop. His timing was good. Woyke had just locked up and
was counting the till. Crake tapped on the window.

Woyke looked up, startled. Reluctantly, he came to the door.
Yes?

I'll just come in if I may.

If you insist.

We'll have a break in our case pretty soon, said Crake when
he was inside.

Ah. Indeed.

I wonder if you would like a bit of protection during the
next week or so.

What? Am I in danger?

No, Mr. Woyke. But I'm bound to ask.

Woyke made a strangled noise which seemed to signify impatience.

Crake nodded toward the open till. Why don't you just go
on with what you were doing? he suggested.

Woyke glanced at the clock, then toward the back room,
then again down at the till. Yes, he said. Yes. Crake settled

himself on a stool nearby. For a few moments the store was quiet while Woyke added up the checks and bills on a pocket calculator. He put them away in a canvas bank bag and as he began to count the silver Crake spoke up.

Business is good since Bill's death?

No.

A pity. I would have thought, after all your years in the business, you'd have had the energy to step in. The trade has all gone to Porres then?

Woyke looked up, scrutinized the Lieutenant's face for a moment, and returned his attention to counting quarters, which he slid off the edge of the counter into his palm two at a time.

No, he said. James is a weak man. He will fail, too.

Will he. You surprise me, Mr. Woyke. I would have thought James was by now quite the master, having had so many opportunities to sit at Bill's feet. More opportunities than yourself, surely. And Bill was the only man to make a living out of the trade, as you said yourself.

I don't believe we are speaking of the same trade, Lieutenant.

Perhaps we aren't. What happens to the till on Saturday? Crake went on after a moment, changing the subject. Woyke had finished counting the coins and was packing some of them into rolls.

Luther can't open the safe, he said. Considering the question of robbery, together with unnecessary temptations, the only course. If the till is above one hundred dollars, he makes a night deposit after closing up. But the till is never that high in the summer. During the season, until New Year's, I work six days a week and so there are no difficulties.

You don't trust him?

It is poor policy to trust people, Lieutenant. An entirely unnecessary test for the boy.

Bill Face took that attitude toward you, I believe.

Woyke's jaw hardened. He zipped up the canvas bag and walked to the back of the store without bothering to reply. Crake heard the door of the safe close and the clicking of the combination as Woyke spun the dial.

Bill and James were close enough, he said when Woyke returned with his hat on. Would you say they trusted each other?

Bill was a very shrewd man, Woyke asserted. James, on the other hand, is a fool. I think it likely James trusted him.

Mm. Are you sure you don't want one of my men for the next week or so?

Their eyes met, which meant that Woyke had to tip his head back. The only sign of tension in him was a slight flaring of the pale nostrils.

I'm leaving now, he said. I'll let you out.

Bit warm for a hat, isn't it?

Woyke snorted. Out on the street, Crake stood for a moment looking across toward Porres's shop.

He intends to sell, I believe, Woyke volunteered.

Yes, so we're told.

Just as well.

Yes.

Good evening, Lieutenant.

Leaving Woyke to wait at the bus stop, Crake stepped diagonally across the street and walked up to the corner. Reaching the patrol car where Tuchman waited, he leaned down and spoke rapidly and briefly.

So far as this evening goes, Frank, I only want to know whether he goes back to the store or directly home. Then you are to continue with your regular duties.

Crake turned slightly, enough to see in the patrol car's mirror that Woyke was watching. Two blocks away, a city bus was just coming off the bridge.

Tomorrow I want you here all day, in uniform. There is no need for subtleties, but don't be particularly obvious, do you understand me? Call me at home tomorrow evening, and report to me Monday morning. I think that will be sufficient. Enjoy the bass fishing, Frank.

Tuchman's face lit up, but Crake walked briskly away before the patrolman could reply. The bus stop was empty. Behind him, the police cruiser jumped hastily to life.

Crake ambled across the street. At the corner he stopped to say a few words to a vagrant sitting in a doorway. The man nodded and got to his feet. Crake went on in the direction of the station. He sat down to rest on a bench at City Hall, shaded by a pomegranate bush. The pomegranates were green, thumb-sized. He closed his eyes and, feeling momentarily for the gun in its holster at his waist, took a few deep breaths.

He would be eligible for early retirement in the fall. Perhaps he ought to take it. As a young man he had never hesitated to smash a case this way, by going for the weakest link. But he had become pernickety. It was a question of aesthetics. An inconvenient and entirely inappropriate pride.

□

The weekend passed without incident, and likewise the week following. Between them, Tuchman and Crake kept Woyke under close observation. On Friday afternoon Crake settled down, not much at ease, for the weekly conference with his Captain.

I've taken Porres off surveillance, said Crake when the Face murder came around for discussion.

The Captain's eyebrows rose slightly, almost imperceptibly, and he tipped his head a bit to one side.

Oh? Pulling back, Milo?

No sir. But it's a waste of time.

Giving him a little rope, then.

Yes sir.

And when was this?

A week ago.

Hmm. Just after our last discussion, in fact, Milo?

Yes sir.

The Captain paused, appraising him dryly. I see you've been making a little extra use of Francis Tuchman, he observed.

Yes sir, Crake replied with embarrassment.

Any good?

Good enough. A bit slow.

Ah. Suits your purposes then, I suppose.

Yes sir.

What was wrong, Milo, with simply shifting our plainclothes man's attention from Porres to Woyke?

Undercover, sir. We want to be seen for this.

Ah. Yes, I see you would. You always have had a knack for scrounging up resources, Milo. I must say, you're a determined bastard.

The two men did not speak for a time. The Captain rose, walked to the window, and returned again to his desk while his subordinate waited to be dismissed.

Milo, he said. I think I understand your, ah, determination. Your view of the importance of this case. I've given you a good deal of discretion because of that. But I think you are getting away with yourself, Milo. You risk compromising the Department.

No, sir. I don't believe so.

Hmm.

The Captain was making no accusations. Crake began to fidgit.

We have some new testimony.

Have you. The Captain's gaze was cool. You haven't said so before this?

Well, you understand we don't actually have a statement, Crake went on, improvising. A tip. Seems to implicate Rufus Woyke.

Does it? Well, that explains your fiddling with the surveillance, I see. Puts a hole in the Porres case, though?

Something of a hole.

The Captain fell silent, looking at the toe of his outstretched boot. He shifted the pictures on his desk slightly, and finally spoke.

That doesn't alter my decision, Milo, he said. Brief one of your men and hand over the paperwork to whoever you like. I'm taking you off this case, Milo. I want you at your desk again on Monday.

Crake prevented himself from protesting.

I can't afford therapy any longer, Milo. I can't afford to indulge you. The Department lacks administrative staff as it is.

Lieutenant Crake set his jaw in anger.

That's all, I think.

Crake went out. In the hall he stopped to think, tapping his shoe on the tile floor just to hear the crisp noise after the muffled sounds of the Captain's office.

So this was the end. He had not counted on having to move so quickly. He had expected to be able to let things soak a week more. But perhaps that could be accommodated. It was only three-thirty. Crake went to his desk. There was time to brief someone, on the Captain's orders. Perhaps it would be a good thing to have another man's testimony now.

He gave orders to have whoever was in the duty room sent in, and left a message for Tuchman there. Then he quickly filled out a search warrant form and called for a runner.

A detective looked in. The young, store-bought sort.

Sit down.

Crake rummaged in his files for a bit. He added a few things from the center drawer of his desk.

That's what we have so far on the Face murder, he said to the man who was still standing, now a few paces from his desk. I'm putting you on it.

Anything pressing?

No. You can look that over on Monday. The man to watch is Rufus Woyke. Owns a bookshop over on Mill Avenue. There's a revolver concerned in it, which hasn't turned up. Seems to belong to Woyke. It's all in the file. I'm going home. Call me if there's trouble.

So that was that, Crake thought as he locked his office door. Rufus Woyke is a wary man. Too wary. He thinks Porres knows something. Perhaps he does. How inconvenient if the new man were to get ambitious, stick his nose in before Monday, spook Woyke prematurely.

The Captain seemed to feel that his Lieutenant's attitude was unreasonable. Was it? Crake supposed it was, in the sense of not alterable by reason. But in the broader sense? He was not certain that he knew what it meant to be not reasoned. He doubted whether he had ever had reasons of that sort in his life, and through he was aware that many people claimed to have, he disdained to pretend, at least to himself. In forty-three years as a policeman he had never been called on to solve a crime by giving thought. The whole system of evidence, forensics, and procedure was designed to avoid the dangerous and uncertain recourse to speculation. Crimes, and murder especially, were completely unintelligible if they were not obvious. The solution was entirely a matter of dog work. That was how he had become a Lieutenant: slowly, doggedly. He was, as the Captain said, an obstinate bastard.

As far as Crake could tell, the store-bought detectives did not proceed much differently. The routine seemed to be the same for everyone. The young ones were not quite so stubborn, and preferred to work in teams, and so they preferred the huge, cumbersome cases which could only be solved by teams, but otherwise the years of study seemed to make no difference in anything but the budget. The system was common because it was effective against common crimes and because anyone could fly it.

Numerous times in his career he had failed the truth, but he had never felt beaten by the unidentified bodies in the desert, the runaway husbands, the mislaid jewelry. Perhaps if he had worked on a mob car bombing, with the anger and stifled justice that mob murders always seemed to produce, he would have learned to deal with some of the things the Porres case threw up at him. Or if he had spent years on a vice squad, with those endless little drug and prostitution bookings, like trying to keep a pile of ping-pong balls on a table.

Crake was a poor loser. The thing that rankled most was that, so far as public opinion was concerned, Porres was likely to be exonerated.

But the Captain had seemed to fear something else in him, too. Crake was aware that there were persons, peculiar persons of large humanity, to whom these things were only sad reminders of human frailty and occasions for human solidarity. And Crake thought that the worst sort of humbug. The reminders, in his experience, were simply excuses for self-indulgence; the occasions, only opportunities for exploitation. He was convinced no one had ever done a thing for entirely the right reasons. At bottom, people are just meat.

Friday night he spent playing video games until nearly dawn: angrily, intensely, victoriously.

He was tired. He was mortally tired, after weeks on his feet, weeks of obsession with the Face murder, weeks of erratic and unsatisfying sleep. That night he collapsed, slept on all through Saturday in the airless apartment, the windows closed, garbage overflowing onto the kitchen floor, and woke, sweating, about five o'clock. He had eaten nothing for almost two days. He felt drained, hammered.

Getting too old for this, he muttered, and rose slowly to his feet. But he had never lived any other way. In two years he would retire. Then what? Nothing, probably. He did not know how to live better.

In the refrigerator he found a half-package of frankfurters, which he ate cold, dipping them into a wide-mouth bottle of catsup. There were also two oranges, which he ate as they were, skin and all. One of the first things that happened to him when he moved here, after the war, was that he got fastidious about citrus fruit. He would eat only local, tree-ripened produce. Now, at the end of May, these were disappearing. There would be no more until Thanksgiving. One of the things he had liked most about his first house was that it had had two orange trees and a grapefruit in the back yard. To him, that was the epitome of living in the desert, to be able to go into the back yard in pajamas on a December morning and pick oranges and grape-fruit for breakfast.

That house, which had been falling down at the time, was razed long ago. He had never had another tree, either.

He also ate apple cores, to the amazement of anyone who saw him do it.

The key, as he understood it, had been Soccorro Porres's silence. Only her father's guilt explained that.

□

Officer Francis Tuchman, wearing a suit that was too heavy for a May evening, and an unfamiliar shoulder holster, sat in Crake's gray government issue car on Terrace Road, just off Greenway, waiting. He had been a patrolman six years. Grade twenty-nine. Bottom of the heap, more or less. Here was a chance to go with

the flyboys in criminal investigations. Instant promotion.
Grade thirty. He wished Lieutenant Crake, grade thirty-six, had
left him alone.

The case was a wrong one. He was in it because he was soft
and stupid, because there was little risk of his opening his
mouth.

Eat what's on your plate. You want to go hungry?

The radio crackled. Got anything, Frank?

No sir.

Crake had taken the handset and gone in on foot. And now
they waited.

Tuchman disliked the business from the beginning. Bill Face
had been one of the big boys, but the sort who remembers your
name and your kid's last illness and wouldn't pick a flower
without first asking after its health. Hard money. Probably
tripped on his prick. That was always how the big boys go, he
was certain. By accident. Fell down and broke his crown. It's
the little ones that get eaten. There was a woman in it somewhere. There's always a woman in it. Jill somebody.

This Woyke was a fey bastard, though. Fragile little alcoholic
sonofabitch, about as friendly as a snake. Woyke was almost
certainly the mark. Woyke and his little turd Luther Idge.
Only Crake knew the inside of the case, of course, and the Captain. Crake had played this one very close. Unusually close,
even for him, they were saying. As if there were something personal in it.

Still, it was a damned flimsy case, from what anyone could
see of it. There was motive and opportunity, but there seemed
to be a lot of that, opportunity being the marginally scarcer
commodity. But none of it would stand up in court. The only
thing that would stand up in court was Woyke's underwear.
Tuchman had an idea most cases were solved this way. Sit
tight, keep your thumb on anyone you don't like, and wait for
the whole thing to curdle.

The radio crackled again, making the Lieutenant's voice
harsh, impatient. Got anything?

Nothing.

Crake was under a bush somewhere up the street. There were

two ways into the neighborhood and Tuchman was posted so as to see both of them. At a moment's warning from Crake he could block either. The back side of the neighborhood was closed off by the freeway.

They waited. Tuchman muttered to himself.

He had been told exactly what to look for: a drab little sedan, thus, thus. He would be in all likelihood too far away, half a block, to tell who was driving. He supposed it would be Woyke. Didn't Woyke always take the bus? But then there was no bus here. Woyke, as Tuchman had heard, was going to buy the farm. There had been a break in the case. Luther Idge had been caught with his hand in the till and had spilled his guts. Porres and Woyke were finished. Catch them with their heads together and it was all over.

So they were saying. Even to Officer Tuchman it was clear what the game was. Woyke was just an excuse. The means and the excuse.

At dusk the car he was looking for appeared around the curve two blocks away and turned into the lane.

OK, he said into the microphone. I've got him. Coming your way. I'm packing up.

Long moments passed before the radio came to life.

He's in. Drop the net.

It wasn't much of an operation, with only the two of them, which contributed to Tuchman's uneasy knowledge of illegitimacy. But more would have been conspicuous in such a small, quiet neighborhood. Tuchman pulled forward onto Carson Drive, blocking the lane. Then he walked back to the other corner, where Greenway debouched onto Carson. That was it. If one of them got past Crake somehow, he would have to get out on foot. Tuchman pulled out the walkie talkie that was clipped to his belt under the hot suit coat.

All set.

There was no reply.

Ahead, Greenway curved off to the left, and halfway along the curve the small brown sedan was parked innocently, guilelessly in front of Porres's house, two wheels up on the sidewalk. From where Tuchman stood the house appeared dark. The carport was empty. Crake had said he would approach from the rear, over the concrete block wall above the freeway.

Tuchman waited, feeling conspicuous. The house on the corner, where he stood, was the only one in sight that was brightly lit, and from the open windows came the sounds of a domestic argument. The two voices rose and fell but never became quite intelligible enough for long enough to tell what the argument was about. Tuchman supposed they were squabbling over money. Everyone he knew squabbled over money and the children. There was nothing else worth it. Whether to go to the mountains or the beach.

Maybe there was something to be said for investigations section after all. Then he would be called into these fights when they were done killing each other instead of meanwhile.

Tuchman looked over the corner house. It was a big place, set well back, with a well-swept rock lawn. Nicely grown eucalyptus and queen palm, and a big bed of annuals. Irrigation system on a timer. Four-wheel drive commando car and a BMW in the driveway. So what on earth were they arguing about? Cat fell in the swimming pool.

You threw it in.

The hell I did.

You did. You hate that cat.

Goddamn right I do. It's evil. Damn thing swims. Look at its eyes! I should have thrown it in, by God.

The woman in the house nearby began to shriek. From down the street came the sound of a shot.

So it was over, Tuchman thought. He started forward gratefully. The woman's voice fell, subsided again into the unintelligible throaty nagging which had been going on for half an hour.

He broke into a run.

□

James Porres turned the little brown sedan onto Carson Drive, then into the lane and onto Greenway Drive. He parked, half up on the walk, in front of his house. It was a small house, for a tri-level, though it had seemed big with only the three of them living in it. He wondered if it would be hard to sell. The realtor, something more to see to next week. It seemed he had a great many more errands than formerly. Perhaps Isela had used to do some of them? That was one the reasons he had begun to use the other car, that had belonged to his daughter. It wasn't much. The upholstery was held together with t-shirts slipped over the seats. But it ran, and Porres was not such a fool as to invest money solely in appearances.

He got out, separating his house key from the others as he walked up the empty driveway, and let himself in the front. The house had been shut up for several weeks and smelled it. Dust. Porres closed the door behind him. Without bothering to turn on the light, he made his way back to his former office to get the files he had come for.

But instead of getting immediately to work, he opened the arcadia doors which led from the workroom out onto the patio. The sound of freeway traffic rushed in from the other side of the block wall at the back of the yard. He leaned against the edge of the open door, one arm over his head, and looked out.

Grief. Porres had always wondered about those Palestinians, ululating on television after some bomb explosion. The women's shrieking was almost a song. And some child's eyes, staring round, violet. He had often wondered about such stylized grief. Was it real?

Hear the voice of my supplications when I cry unto thee, when I lift up my hands . . .

Some traditional lamentation, some faithful love song. No one talks that way anymore. But did they ever?

Hear me, I am a poor Jew . . .

Make haste, oh God, to deliver me. Make haste to help me, oh Lord. Let them be ashamed and confounded that seek after my soul. Let them be turned back that say aha! aha!

The front door opened. The sound reached Porres easily through the quiet house, a metallic snick easily audible over the formless hissing of freeway traffic. A breeze, drawn in through the open patio door, lifted the papers on his desk.

Long moments passed. The intruder, apparently unfamiliar with the house, was conducting a systematic search. Porres listened for the hiss of the man's feet on the carpet. The intruder paused in a doorway, brushed lightly against a wall.

Silence. Porres turned around slowly, calmly.

The man, only a thick shadow in the darkness, raised his hand slightly as if in greeting, and stepped forward.

Hello, Lieutenant.

The policeman's revolver was in his hand. Porres forced his eyes away from the gun, up to Lieutenant Crake's face. The older man was smiling a little, dryly, but he said nothing. The muscles of his jaw and neck tensed slightly and his eyelids fell, slowly closing.

A light flashed from the patio behind Porres, with a sound like a hammer falling on a tin roof. Crake's head drew back a little, as if he had felt a twinge in his neck, the beginnings of a cramp. His lips drew in between his teeth. Without speaking a word he fell back, crumpled to the floor. Once, weakly, he raised his other, empty hand. Then he was still.

The gunman on the patio began to laugh, at first the soft giggling of a lover, then more derisive. Rufus Woyke stepped forward, an aluminum-colored pistol in his hand. He looked curiously at the little hole which his bullet had ripped in the screen before stepping inside to kneel down and put his ear to Crake's chest.

Porres, dumbfounded, did nothing. Woyke rose to his feet again, nodding.

Dead.

Woyke's voice was solemn. Later, Porres thought it was the first time he had heard anything that might really be called awful.

Woyke looked into Porres's eyes once briefly, fiercely, and slipped out. Then he was gone the way he had come, over the wall and down the freeway embankment.

Tuchman appeared in the doorway, dressed in an unfamiliar gray suit.

It was April again: spring. A year had passed since the death of Bill Face. Caitlin's unhappiness had been growing slowly through the autumn and winter and was by now a thick bush, well able to withstand a summer drought. This desert gardening. One has to provide everything: water, shade, fertilizer, iron, acid, trace minerals. Even dirt.

It wasn't simply a case of miscarriage of justice, if that's what it had been. She was hardened enough to expect miscarriages of justice now and then. Perhaps even frequently. She supposed it might be a frequent occurrence.

Nor was it an absence of satisfying answers. There are, she knew, people who are driven mad by such things. Rarely did they become policemen. Luckily for them. At least, she supposed rarely. They wouldn't stick it if they did. Having things neat is more of an accountant's motivation.

How could she go on about motivation when plainly she knew nothing about it?

But then, who knew any better? The police did not. They had been coming to no conclusions about the motivation of the murderer while she, Caitlin Vachon, had been coming to no conclusions about herself.

Perhaps the difficulty was in wanting conclusions, in wanting things sewed up, complete. Wasn't that anti-life, somehow? Bill Face was sewed up, complete. Through no fault of his own, as it appeared. But there are, she knew, people who are upset by the prospect of such a life, inconclusive and emptied of purpose. Of great purposes, at least: greater than themselves, than going to the store for milk. Absent explanations are like absent parents who might, after all, have abandoned you . . .

But there are things mysterious because unknown, as distinct from things unknowable. Is there really a heavy boson? Which

141

ought to be answerable with the right machine. What is the cause of evil? Which also ought to be answerable, if we can find the right grown-up to ask.

Caitlin remembered a time when she disbelieved in evil, believed only in well-meaning ignorance. A kind of everyday evil. She was comforted by the absence of great purposes. By a low-profile humanity. Perhaps she was having a spiritual crisis? And how would she propose to resolve the question of purpose? Would she prefer a world simple enough to be understood by human intelligence? Could there be human intelligence in such a world?

Probably simple curiosity was a sufficient explanation. Not necessary or complete, but sufficient. With lingering doubts. Low-tech detection.

Is unsatisfied curiosity, by itself, sufficient to explain an emotional disease? Probably: if anything can be an explanation, it probably is. Curiosity, as is well known, kills.

But one wants more of an explanation than that. At least, some people do. Simple emotions (curiosity, neatness, ignorance) are not part of the great events and high deeds which alone ought to reveal the meaning of life. The drama. Ought not be part of it, anyway. If there is to be drama.

Small feelings, small time.

Low-tech life.

Everyday life, which doesn't explain diddly-squat, which everyone is in a hurry to depart. As quickly as possible. For something better.

At one time she had thought the world had lost grandeur. But it isn't that there are no great things, it's that great things are built up, gradually, from little things. The disease of her accountant's soul was not that it was offended by a world out of balance (and it was offended) but that it remained so obstinately unconvinced that great numbers were anything more than just numbers.

She needed to begin looking at common little things in a new way. She needed to stop demanding that events mean something. When she did stop . . .

□

Caitlin wanted to talk to Porres again. She wanted to clear everything up, to see whether it could be cleared up.

That was not so easy. He had moved. His telephone number was unlisted. Everything he touched had been transferred to receivers, box numbers, or anonymity of some other sort. The bookshop was gone, replaced by a management company the officers of which were as anonymous as Porres himself. The company was charged with overseeing Bill Face's redevelopment property. Caitlin wondered how much else of Bill's business had come into Porres's hands by now. All he had needed was an opening. He had inherited nothing. In the year since Bill's death he had only picked up what was lying about. Never in a way to arouse suspicion, not ostentatiously, not surreptitiously.

For several weeks, insofar as she was able, Caitlin kept a stake-out on the condominium to which she traced him before, but without success. She kept an eye on his management company, and made the discreetest of inquiries that she was legally capable of among the banks and brokers. But finally she had to turn again to Luther Idge.

Try the canal near Indian Bend and Granite Reef, he said.

She had found him working in a garage down on the river, salvaging parts from junk cars. The manager's call brought him to the shop door.

Hi yo, he shouted, grinning good-naturedly and wiping his hands on his greasy shirt. What's doin?

Nothing much. You keeping your eyes open?

Sure am. The bigger they are the more they got to lose.

Make sure you don't burn yourself, Luther.

Sure enough.

He put out his greasy hand, but then thought better of it and, strolling back out to the yard, he flung her a wink and a leer, drawing whistles from the men who had been watching avidly in the shadows of the gloomy, cavernous shop.

You hold your end up, peckerwood, Caitlin shouted after him, raising a whoop that reverberated from the metal roof.

That afternoon she drove out to the area of the canal that

Luther had suggested. For the moment she had no idea what to do next, or why this particular place was of significance. The directions were not especially good. Granite Reef Road came to an end on the south side of the canal without reaching an intersection with Indian Bend; its continuation north of the canal was named 84th Street. Caitlin supposed he had meant streets and not other features—there did not appear to be another conjunction of a canal and anything appropriately named. She spent an hour driving slowly along the streets in the neighborhood of the canal, wishing she had brought a map. The south side was a well-to-do development of large, close-packed, one- and two-story houses with shake roofs, solar water heaters, and a good view of Camelback Mountain to the west. On the north side of the canal was open ground, a stable and exercise yard for horses, and a few unimproved streets of custom houses: low, flat-roofed buildings of pink or tan stucco seemingly made up from a dozen or so large square chimneys and covered with honeysuckle, bougainvillea, and acacia. Caitlin parked for a while at the end of 84th and looked out toward the canal five hundred yards off.

When she emerged again onto Hayden Road it was with the idea of going home. But she could not stand to give up her only lead yet, and on impulse she turned off into a small park built beside the canal where it passed under Hayden Road. She got out of the car and went to sit on a picnic table under a ramada, with her feet up on a barbecue grill, and think. In front of her were the two neighborhoods she had vainly explored, with the canal curving off to the right between them. A high wooden fence ran along the south side of the canal, leaving a gravel service road ten feet wide, blocked at the intersection with Hayden Road by a chain. Around the bend of the canal, half a mile away, an elderly couple on a tandem bicycle appeared, pedaling slowly. At the near end of the same tow path a lean middle-aged man in running clothes stepped over the chain and jogged easily away. A similar tow path ran along the other side of the canal, dropping off to the north into a strip of gray scrub desert.

To the north-east the ground fell away gradually, the canal marking an isocline through the folds and barren hummocks at the foot of McDowell Mountain ten miles off, and then rose again in successive ridges to the Mazatzal Range and beyond, the Mogollon Rim. It was a day of crystalline dry air. The mountains stepped back into the distance in separate bands of ever deeper purple, at last obscured by haze and blended smoothly into the equally indistinct sky. The date palms and eucalyptus of the valley ended at the foot of these terraced mountains, giving way to cactus and cat's claw scrub, a wash of faint green on the distant purple slopes. On such a spring day it seemed as if she could see to the end of the universe, where the light swooped up into the sky and curved back on itself, beginning its long return.

Behind her lay the ridge of Camelback Mountain, below it the rubble of Indian Bend Wash and then a jumble of half-million dollar desert houses rising to the foot of the mountain itself. Bill Face's house had been there. On late nights he had stood pensively in a window, a drink in his hand, gazing out over the spangles of orange light in this little nook of the valley to the blackness of the reservation and the mountains beyond.

Nearest Caitlin in that direction, a quarter of a mile away over the wash, was an immense condominium, huge blocks of violet-colored, ten-story buildings each faced with hundreds of rococo balconies. Finally, to the northwest, lay the open expanse of the McCormick Ranch golf course on the low ground stretching away along the wash.

She had no idea yet what to do. Somewhere in this panorama was the man she sought. She assumed that he lived here, but even without considering the condominium, which was really nowhere near Granite Reef Road or the canal, the area was far too large and thickly populated to survey directly. She could go to the tax rolls, but there was no reason to suppose that Porres's name would appear, boldly. Some faceless investment company it would be.

Hadn't she been up here once before on business for Porres? Yes, when looking for Luther Idge the first time. The address on his business license had been in the McCormick Ranch area just to the north. Caitlin had wondered at the time how Luther had been able to get in there. Suppose it were some property

of Bill's, that he had exploited temporarily, through Porres?
That was nowhere the canal, but perhaps there were other of
Bill's old properties in this neighborhood that Porres had ac-
quired.

A second jogger appeared on the canal path, approaching
from around the bend, and suddenly Caitlin's mind slipped. If
Porres lived here, perhaps he could be caught on the canal paths.
It was possible that Luther's knowledge was no more than this,
that he had seen Porres out for a run along here.

The weather was beginning again to turn warm. Caitlin
guessed that her best chance to catch Porres lay in the cool
morning before work, and every morning for a week she left
her apartment at four-thirty for the hour's drive north, lying
in wait or walking the canal path until she had to return, an
hour and a half through rush-hour traffic into the city and work
by nine o'clock, without breakfast. Her guess was correct. On
the first morning of the second week she found James Porres.

She first saw him fifty yards off, running slowly toward her,
his head down. She was leaning casually, still unnoticed, against
the fence when he passed.

Hello, James.

Porres stopped and turned, recognizing her after a brief moment, acknowledging her with a slight bow, without surprise.

Caitlin.

Then he went on. She broke away and paced him along the
canal path with easy strides. They ran east, away from the
road. For a time neither spoke. She looked at Porres who ran
beside her, so short, three steps to her two, but moving without
effort. He had completed the transformation begun at Bill's
death: no longer pudgy and white, prominently bald. Money
and leisure and exercise had made him lithe, weathered. And he
had grown a moustache, which he waxed into arrogant points.

So, Porres observed, you are still interested in the murder
after all this time. Is it just unsatisfied curiosity, or do you
hope to prove something?

Curiosity.

I would think so.

Porres had plainly put himself into excellent condition. He showed no strain, spoke easily. Caitlin was already beginning to pant a bit.

Is there anything new? Porres inquired, pleasantly, as between friends who had not met in six months.

No. Nothing new.

It doesn't surprise me. There never is anything new, is there?

That had not changed, at least, his trick of turning simple questions into general inquiries. She took him up. It's an illusion, she said.

Do you think so, Caitlin?

What are you told by the newspapers, James? Mysterious death. Several suspects. Franz Kafka arrested. Then you never hear of it again. If they don't manage to hang it on Kafka, the continuation is on page ten of the local news. I don't know about you, but I always finish my grapefruit before I get to page ten.

Yes, so do I. But you do like things neat, Caitlin. Of course you are no farther along than you were a year ago. People aren't so easily explained as that.

There are explanations, though. Some murders are solved eventually, even on page ten.

Yes, it would appear so.

Caitlin was getting tired, falling behind the pace. She lengthened her stride a little. Porres went on talking easily.

Are you never suspicious, he inquired, when a murder is solved suddenly, after a year or two of inquiries among the dogs and cats? Look at the present instance. All are suspected, but none is called. Why? It can't be for lack of a motive. Some people's reasons are only a little more obscure. One can always find a motive. A motive proves nothing. Envy, ambition. Unassuming people often find a hidden streak of ambition in themselves as they get older. Was I sufficiently envious? Sufficiently ambitious? How to decide? And what of greed, resentment? Such mean emotions. So small. Are they to weigh more than my large, copious envy? Or is it that Rufus Woyke, being small and mean, is better suited as a murderer? How to decide? The police, I'm told, pay little attention to motive. Sensible of them.

James, do you really think all answers are either obvious or wrong?

Certainly I do. Our friend Rufus's maladroitness has caused him to be left holding the bag. This is convenient all around, but pleases no one. And unfortunately, for lack of evidence he cannot be tried. So he is put away on the other charge instead, of killing Lieutenant Crake. Justice is served, the police are revenged, but everyone feels cheated. And what is to be done? It is fortunate for us that justice is so easily satisfied.

Caitlin was falling behind again. She took several deep breaths and let her arms fall to her sides.

You see how explanations proliferate, Porres went on. It seems there was a good bit of coming and going at the back of the shop that night, but the details cannot be brought into focus. Perhaps if it were treated as a problem in statistics? You have the mathematics for that, don't you, Caitlin? But then, one can't be convicted on probability. Bill was in the habit of stopping by when he needed cash, and that may have been his business that night. There is no evidence of his intentions. I was aware of Bill's habit, you know, before the police brought it to my attention. They were hoping to embarrass me, I suppose. It did put me in a bad light. Bill started it years ago. I find it hard to remember the petty inconveniences of that time, before bank cards and automatic tellers and all. Bill paid none of that any attention, even before he had money. He wouldn't be troubled to stand in line. Anything which requires waiting a turn, he would say, can't be worthwhile.

Commonplace. Vulgar.

No. Bill was quite a common person, and I don't think I ever heard him say anything against the working class. No, simply boring. Bill was a complete hedonist. Now then. What do you really know about what happened the night he died? Nothing. It seems he fell off a ladder.

Caitlin stumbled and recovered.

Lieutenant Crake had a number of theories, some more fun than others. You have been able to add a few to the list, no doubt. But there is no evidence, no *evidence*, for anything but accidental death.

Caitlin was by now winded. Between breaths she complained that the evidence shouldn't have been fudged if Bill had only fallen off a ladder.

Fear, Porres replied, explains much.

So does curiosity.

Porres gazed at her for a moment, unsmiling. It was the Lieutenant's strategy, he said then, to attack with any weapon at hand, quickly, while everyone was off balance. Quite a good tactic in this case, actually. It might have worked. There is no reason why it should not have succeeded.

They had come to the point where the canal path entered the Salt River Reservation. Here it was blocked by a chain. The canal continued on beyond the chain, between the cotton field and the open desert. Porres stopped. Caitlin, flowing with sweat, bent over, hands on her knees, trying to get her breath.

Opportunity, then, Porres went on. I had quite enough opportunity, but then so did anyone. The question of witnesses and so forth is unfortunately subject to luck. Who has an alibi for two o'clock in the morning? At that hour, in a suburban town, witnesses and excuses are, not surprisingly, scarce. Especially if husband and wife have separate beds, separate rooms, separate lives.

Caitlin struggled to breathe. Porres watched her gasping for a moment, coldly.

If Bill's death had been investigated, you know, by someone —a time-server, or a more forgiving man—none of this would have happened.

Caitlin straightened slowly, feeling lightheaded and weak. She raised her eyes, gazed out into the distance toward the young, naked, unweathered mountains. She had nothing to say.

I believe I'm actually in Lieutenant Crake's debt, Caitlin. I admit it, Porres went on, smiling. If Crake had not squeezed me so hard I would undoubtedly have remained as I was.

Why not as you were? What was wrong with that?

Porres shrugged. I was poor, he said, and changed the subject.

Do you think, when so much effort is invested in the solution of a murder, that any answer is not a little unsatisfactory? We feel instinctively that the truth is an elegant thing, and if things are as difficult and inelegant as this they cannot be true. Or ought not to be. Rather, the truth has been obscured in some way by our own ignorance, obtuseness. We are not very intelligent creatures. I have never been much impressed by a struggle against great odds. Anything that difficult must have been botched at the start. Only the stupidest people struggle against great odds. Others find ways to reduce the odds.

Not much for heroes, are you, James?

Porres shrugged again. I'm weak, Caitlin. If answers come easily doesn't that seem rather convenient for everyone? Doesn't that leave a few too many illusions standing? The weaker and the stupider we are, the harder the answers, the more we cry for heroes and the less likely we are to get them.

Caitlin did not reply. Porres seemed amused. He pointed back along the path up which they had come to the slope of Camelback Mountain visible above the housetops.

Bill's house was up in there, he said. I imagine he looked down here quite a bit. In the evenings, you know. A log burning in the fireplace, a drink, quiet music. The valley is achingly beautiful at night, when the air is clear, isn't it? Bill was quite sensitive to beauty, whereas I haven't the eye. A shame.

She thought Porres was teasing her. He was so at ease, with his little smiles and sidelong glances and catlike questions. The sweat was drying on her and she was beginning to feel cold.

Do you know, Caitlin, that I was once quite the mystic. I remember riding to work on my bicycle thinking about the intricate design of the world. Riding a bicycle encourages that, I've found. I knew nothing of little things, of everyday life, everyday pain. I was fond of biological explanations which revealed the interconnectedness of things. Individual will meant nothing to me. Living here in the desert encourages that sort of viewpoint, I think. It's a peculiar religion, but it is a religion. Clear light, vast space, eremites and aridity. The desert encourages one in the belief that the truth will be made manifest to the fortunate, the persistent, the clear-sighted.

And have you changed so much?

Oh, not at all. A bit hardened, perhaps. Fewer expectations.

But you know, it *is* astonishing how quickly people will change their views under pressure. You would think we had no principles at all. People are really inexplicable. To say otherwise demeans us.

That's a neat trick, James. It puts the onus on the talkers, eh? A pretty good businessman's philosophy.

Porres gazed at her with deep contempt. You suppose, he said, that the truth will make you free and pure and that sort of thing?

The question was left hanging between them in silence for a long time.

Well, Porres said at last. The light tone had not returned to his voice. Lieutenant Crake tried to make a case against me and failed. Why, I don't know.

Why he wanted to, or why he failed?

Both. Now you take up the charge, for reasons just as mysterious to me, and perhaps also to yourself. And you've failed, likewise. But you stupidly persist. I've watched you at this for a year.

Have you?

First Crake, then you. I see the prospect of an infinite series of detectives, each with a vendetta, forever unsuccessful. None will prove me guilty, none innocent.

There will be spiritual heirs on both sides, I imagine.

Yes. I should push you into the canal, I suppose. Shouldn't I? Break the chain.

You'd rather be guilty than uncertain?

Porres snorted. I'm a man of business, as you say.

Business and religion have a lot in common.

I don't understand this eagerness for religion. They want the certainty, they say. The security. Can't they see how arbitrary and vicious their gods are?

It's better than no gods at all, I suppose.

Taking matters into one's own hands is always preferable.

He gave Caitlin a long and penetrating look, which she returned with difficulty. At last his eyes fell. To his hands, which he began to flex as if they were cold.

I've risen since Bill's death. Or rather it's as if he moved aside for me. That would be quite like him. No credit to him, of course. No credit to anyone.

Porres had been leaning against one of the posts to which the chain was attached which blocked the path. Now he stood up, bouncing a little on the balls of his feet to get the blood circulating again, to stretch his legs gone a little stiff.

Out of curiosity, Caitlin, would you prefer your death to be a clean, aesthetic one or a bloody apotheosis?

The aesthetic one, I think.

Yes, said Porres. I thought so. The desert is a hostile place. Life here is precarious, fragile, artificial. We haven't any right, really. We should go humbly, quietly. I quite agree.

After a moment's further reflection, Porres ran easily away, back to wherever he had come from, leaving Caitlin at the end of the path. The sun was well up now. She would be late for work.

Tired already, she trudged back along the canal, which carried water out of the desert, to her car.

March 1985